STRONGHOLD

STRONGHOLD

ANA ASHLEY

HeartEyes Press

For those who travel to find themselves not realizing the destination can be closer to home than you think. The bumps and bruises you gain along the way make the return that much sweeter.

JUDSON

The steam rising from the coffee in front of me swirls up to fill my senses with its delicious promise of caffeinated goodness.

It's still too hot to drink, and I remember my first class at culinary school, where I learned how to brew the perfect coffee.

The class was filled with bleary-eyed students who'd been out the night before and dying to drink the coffee, but instead, we were asked to stare at it, slow down...focus.

Despite the sleep deprivation, it was one of the most valuable lessons I learned. One I try to channel every time the ghosts of the past come chasing. Every time I missed home.

Well, I am home now.

Outside, the rising sun teasing beyond the tree line tells me that, despite the familiarity, I'm not where I'm supposed to be. The fresh layer of snow covering the backyard confirms the same. After all, this is Vermont.

Mud season is around the corner, but for now, the pristine white is still king.

I take a sip of the coffee, allowing the bitterness to reach my tastebuds before making its way down to settle in my stomach.

If I don't look outside the window, maybe I can pretend that the temperatures aren't subzero and that, at six-thirty in the morning, it's still too early for the sun to rise.

"Morning, honey. What are you doing up so early?" my mom asks, stepping into the kitchen wearing the same terrycloth bathrobe that I swear she's worn for the last twenty years. And it smells the same too. Lavender, honey, and home.

I put my arms around her waist when she comes closer and kisses the top of my head. How is it possible that it feels like I've never left, but at the same time, even in the house I grew up in, I'm an alien transported from a different world?

How can I miss this but also wish I wasn't here?

"Hey, Mom. Couldn't sleep. I'm used to being up early, and I guess I'm over the jet lag now." I get up and grab a clean cup from the cabinet to pour fresh coffee for her while she goes into the pantry, coming back with a bag of flour and a packet of dry yeast.

"I was about to get the bread started, but do you want me to whip you up a batch of pancakes?" she asks.

"You know I won't say no to your pancakes, Mom." Even though I probably should because it's been too cold to go out for a run, and I can feel the weight piling back on every time I walk past the kitchen and smell whatever my mom is cooking.

My mom has always loved to cook for us, a passion I know I got from her, but the looks I've gotten from my dad and brother tell me she's dialed it up a hundred notches since I came home. Not that anyone will complain. My mom's cooking is the best.

"Righty-o, I'll get started on the pancakes, and you can get started on the bread," she orders, returning to the pantry.

"Oh my, how things have changed around here," I tease. "In the old days, you'd never have let me in the kitchen before I was washed, dressed, and ready for school."

"You're twenty-eight. I trust that you do all those things without needing to be told. Besides, I don't have a Cordon Bleu-trained chef at home for nothing." She's full of pride, but to me, it's like a rock weighing me down.

I give her a smile that I don't feel. At this moment, my Cordon Bleu training isn't worth the paper my certificate is printed on.

There's no point thinking about things I can't change, so I focus on what I *can* do instead. And that's a mean white loaf.

We work in silence. The rest of the house is still asleep but won't be for long. My dad will be up soon. He likes working late into the night, so he rarely gets up earlier than the time he needs to get ready and grab a coffee to go before he heads off.

On the other hand, my little brother may need a cattle prod to get him out of bed. I remind myself that Luke isn't so little anymore. He was five when I left and, despite the regular video calls, it was still a shock to hug a tall, pimply younger version of me when I came back a week ago.

The only difference between us is that when I was fifteen, I definitely did not have the slim frame with long limbs that seem to have graced my sports-inclined younger brother's genetic makeup.

I put the dough in a bowl to rise and cover it with plastic wrap just as mom places a plate with a stack of pancakes on the table, along with a fresh pot of coffee.

"They smell divine, Mom." I grab two plates from the cabinet as she brings our empty coffee cups from the counter to the table.

My stomach rumbles. I'm used to grabbing a piece of fruit on my way to the gym or before a run first thing in the morning, but my lack of exercise in the last week, together with a change in my eating routine, is definitely giving my body ideas I don't want it to have.

I place two pancakes on my plate and dig in.

"Is that it?" Mom asks.

"What do you mean?"

"You used to stack them in piles of at least four with a generous serving of butter and maple syrup."

I look down at my plate of dry pancakes and back at her. She looks...disappointed?

"No, never mind," she says. "You're a grown man now. You've

3

outgrown your childhood habits, right? I'm sure people in Paris are all sophisticated and proper, and you're used to—"

"Mom."

She places her hand on top of mine and squeezes it. "I'm really happy you're home, Judson."

I nod and smile because I don't have the guts to say anything else.

Every day since I arrived I've waited for the moment either of my parents asks how long I'm staying, what am I really doing here, and the absolute worst, what happened?

Dad rushes into the kitchen with the energy of a man thirty years younger and kisses my mom while grabbing her ass.

I look away, trying my best to keep my pancakes inside my stomach. I'd forgotten how in love and open about it my parents still are.

That's how it is, right? When you find the person you're meant to be with for the rest of your life.

I drink the last of my coffee, wondering how the list of topics I don't want to think about keeps getting longer and longer in my head.

"Morning, Judson." He squeezes my shoulder before filling his to-go coffee cup and leaving again.

"I'm going to wake up your brother. If you hear screaming, it's all perfectly normal. No need to call the neighbors or police," Mom says as she leaves me to check on my beautifully risen dough.

True enough, there are knocks on doors, grunts, and doors opening and shutting before the sound of the longest shower in the history of showers. I definitely do not miss being a teenager.

By the time Luke comes down, my bread is out of the oven and cooling on the countertop. The kitchen smells just like a home should in the morning.

My stupid brain brings back the last good memory I have with Pierre. Him walking into the kitchen of our Paris apartment, wearing nothing but a pair of black boxer shorts. The elastic band

4

low on his hips perfectly showcasing his toned abs, his morning wood at half-mast but ready to go at a moment's notice, as it always was.

The memory is swiftly followed by a less pleasant one. I snap out of it quickly, but my mom's worried expression as she looks at me tells me I've been caught.

"Why don't you go out for a walk, sweetheart? Get some fresh air, maybe see your friends. Have you caught up with—?"

"No." I interrupt sharply and then feel like a dick for it. "Sorry, Mom. I didn't mean...I'm just not up for seeing anyone."

She leans against the kitchen sink and crosses her arms. There it is, her signature move.

"Let's put it this way, you either get your butt outside and work that mopey look off your face, or you can kiss goodbye all of your favorite dinners. God knows Luke has his own ideas on what I should feed you all."

"Damn right. Since you got here, we've been eating like it's Sunday every day. I'm not complaining, but Coach Allen will bench me if I can't jump hoops," he says, but it doesn't stop him from stuffing his face with at least a quarter of the bread loaf. Where the fuck does he put all his food?

"Fine, I'll go outside," I say, resigned to my sentence of death by frostbite. At least if I'm dead and in heaven, I can have all of my favorite mom-made food without needing to worry about the carb-to-protein ratio.

The first thing I do when I get to my room is check my phone. No messages or missed calls from Pierre.

Paris is six hours ahead, and I left a week ago. Even considering how much time he spends at the restaurant, I don't believe for one moment he hasn't had the time to contact our lawyer.

I send him a reminder email and put the phone down again to find something warm to wear.

One benefit of all the weight I lost after I left home is that I don't have to search too deep into my old closet to find a Vermont winter-proof coat that fits me.

I still feel like I'm knocked sideways as soon as I step outside. I'm definitely not acclimatized to Vermont winters anymore. I wrap my scarf tighter around my face and steel myself before I walk down the porch steps and onto the fresh snow, following the literal footprints my dad and Luke left behind earlier.

"Judson, honey?" my mom calls from the door. "If you make it all the way to Church Street, would you get us a box of crullers from The Maple Factory? It's Thursday."

I don't know why it being Thursday matters, but I don't question it. I also haven't thought of where my walk is going to take me, but Burlington isn't that big a place, so I know whatever route I take, I'll be close enough to Church Street that I can swing past.

The longer I walk, the more familiar I am with the feel of the snow crunching beneath my feet. Pierre goes skiing every year. It's the one vacation he has without me because it reminds me too much of home. Correction, the one vacation he had without me.

Now I wonder if he wasn't exactly on his own when he was up in the French Alps.

Damn my fucking brain.

I don't know what's next in my life. If I still have a career worth saving or a chance of still doing what I was born to do, but thinking about the past doesn't do anyone any good.

Okay, new plan. Well, only plan. I need to pick myself up and move on.

Church Street has changed since I was last here. There are more stores and restaurants than I remember, and even under these ridiculous freezing conditions, there are still so many people around.

I slow my pace, taking everything in. It doesn't feel as cold now that I've been walking. Or maybe I've just lost all my toes and fingers to frostbite and haven't realized it yet.

Either way, I channel my old teacher and just…appreciate. It's not like I have anywhere better to be or anything better to do.

The recent snowfall covers the brick street, so I'm careful where I place my feet. The last thing I need is to slip or trip over something and, as my friend Spencer says in his very British accent, fall arse over tit to the ground.

The large building that once housed the hostel on Church Street is boarded up. The windows of the upper floors are covered in black soot. There must have been a fire.

The Maple Factory seems to have a line of people spilling outside onto the street. Next door, there's a large brick building with a neon sign that says Vino and Veritas.

As I get closer, to avoid The Maple Factory line, I notice that Vino and Veritas are, in fact, two businesses. On one side, there's a bookstore, and on the other, there seems to be a bar.

My little gay heart jumps for joy at the sight of the rainbow flags in the windows. Burlington has always been a welcoming place for the LGBT community, but I can't recall having such an open space available for socializing.

The line is going strong at The Maple Factory, and I notice an intriguing book display of *The Foodie's Guide to Vermont* in the bookstore window, so I decide to wait out the line in the warmth.

As I go in through the shared entrance, I see a Help Wanted sign in the closed bar door. I snap a quick photo before going inside the bookstore.

Twenty minutes later, I leave the bookstore very impressed with their selection of cookbooks and with a copy of *The Foodie's Guide to Vermont* in my hand.

I join the much smaller line to The Maple Factory just as my phone dings with a message.

Monsieur Pascal advised the paperwork could take a minimum of thirty days to complete. Are you sure you want to do this? It's not too late.

2

SKYLER

"Hey, Ma. Have I told you how much I love you recently?" I say, walking into the kitchen and wrapping my arms around my mother's tiny frame.

"Not since this morning, and I'm pretty sure the scrambled eggs and bacon had something to do with it."

I put a hand to my chest, feigning shock. "Mother. I would never."

Her hands go to her hips, and she tilts her head. "So you're saying the pulled pork I'm about to take out of the oven and the maple syrup barbecue sauce I have to go with it are not the reasons you're declaring your love?"

"Did you make fresh buns?" I ask.

She gasps. "Who do you take me for, Skyler West? Of course there are freshly made buns."

"Damn, woman, have I told you today how much I love you?" my dad says, coming into the kitchen from the back door.

"No, and you'd do well to follow your son's example," she says. "Although I'd like to see how much love there would be in this household if, heaven forbid, I didn't cook for a day."

And just like we've done countless times, Dad and I stand on either side of my mom and kiss her cheeks.

She pushes us both away, and we laugh. "Off you go. I want you both cleaned up for dinner and back here in twenty minutes."

We both take a salute and disappear upstairs.

My muscles relax under the hot shower. Last week's sudden drop in temperature and subsequent snow brought forth the work I'd been putting off for a couple of weeks.

With the cows inside most of the day, Dad and I spent the week fixing fences, strengthening weak spots, cutting wood, and everything else you could possibly imagine related to fences.

It's always so easy to forget how much land we really own because we only use a quarter of it. Still, the cows have free rein, and that means *a lot* of fences. Fucking fences.

I run the soap over my body, wishing not for the first time that I had someone to share the shower with. Someone that could work the knots on my back loose while paying attention to other areas, too.

"There's always tonight," I say, looking down at my half-hard dick.

I'm only going for a few drinks with my friends, but there's always a chance of meeting someone new at Vino. It's not the same as being in a steady relationship, but it meets a very important life need. Beggars can't be choosers, right?

It's not like I have much time to date someone properly. As my ex-boyfriend, Theo, accurately described, anyone who wants to be with me needs to accept cows and trees come first.

His face as he stared at me the day we broke up is still etched into my mind. The way his piercing brown eyes framed by the long lashes demanded I give him the answer he wanted. He wanted his statement to either shock me or change me. It didn't.

Not that our month-long relationship could really be called a relationship, but it was the closest I've been to trying it out for size. I learned my lesson.

And that's why it's much easier to score the occasional hookup who won't care that I've spent the day cleaning cow shit, fixing fences, or cleaning my equipment in readiness for the maple-tapping season.

I get out of the shower and dress quickly, running downstairs just in time to avoid being scolded by the most important woman in my life.

"Dad, I've lined up Francis to help you out next week. Four hours per day," I say.

He looks at me. "Why? Where are you going?"

I sigh. I'm going where I always go, to work on my own business, which he seems to think should come second to his.

"Tapping season is coming up, Dad. Gotta make sure I'm all ready for it."

He grunts but says nothing else. Mom looks at me with an understanding smile.

The farm isn't mine. It's not my dream, and it's not what I want to do with my life, but until my brother finishes college and his work placement at a dairy farm in Wisconsin, I'm more or less stuck helping my dad out.

Miles was born to follow in our dad's footsteps. As a kid, I wanted nothing more than to leave home and travel the world until I figured out what I wanted to do. My brother only ever wanted to be around cows and milk. He still does.

I still remember the day he was first allowed to help my dad out on the farm. He came home and proudly announced that he'd named all the cows and spent the duration of our dinner reciting them. I've never seen my dad look so proud.

Fortunately, we're a dairy farm rather than a cattle farm, or I'm pretty sure he'd have us all turn vegetarian.

After dinner, my dad goes off to watch a game on TV while I help my mom clean up.

"You know he doesn't mean it, don't you?" she says, looking out to the living room to make sure Dad doesn't overhear us talking. If he does, he'll want to know if we're talking about him.

"What? To talk about my business as if it's nothing but a

hobby? To expect me to work for free while I'm standing in for Miles?"

She puts the dishcloth down and gives me a tight hug.

"Maybe if you told him how successful you are. I met Audrey Fletcher in town the other day. She said she saw your maple syrup on sale all the way out in Montpellier."

"That was meant to be a surprise," I say. "I was going to tell you. I've been sending out samples of Maple Sky to different places, and so far, I've secured the exclusive supplier position for a shop in Montpellier and another in Colebury."

"I'm so proud of you, honey."

I run my hands down her arms and then clutch her hands. "Dad can't know."

"I know." I understand the resignation in her voice, but it's too risky.

My dad isn't a bad person, but he's an addict. We nearly lost everything we have once, and I won't let it happen again.

Even though my *side business* turns over as much as the farm, I can't tell him. Not until Miles is back and can officially take over the farm, including its finances.

"Nine months, Ma. The same time it takes for a calf to grow inside its momma. That's how long we have to wait until Miles is back home. Then we can tell Dad."

"All right, baby. Now, tell me about tonight. You meeting someone special?"

I laugh. "Nah, Ma. Just the guys. A couple of drinks, and I'll be back home, in bed, trying to work out the kinks in my back from running after Florrie today."

"What happened?"

"That cow seems to think she's some kind of pet or that she owns the place. I accidentally left the gate open earlier when I was cleaning the stalls, and she escaped. Fortunately, she's no leader. Or maybe the others aren't followers, but I only had to contend with the one great escapee."

She squeezes my hand and smiles. She knows I was never cut

out to be a dairy farmer. Ever since I can remember, while my younger brother was obsessed with cows, I was obsessed with the world.

Vermont was too small for my young mind. I wanted to see the big cities people can get lost in, and I wanted to see the beach, a real one where you can swim in the ocean.

I never thought that my father's biggest betrayal to his family would also lead to me discovering a new dream. That maybe I was always meant to stay here, but instead of looking after cows, I'm looking after trees.

Trees that were here way before my grandfathers and my great-grandfathers. Trees that are kind enough to bleed that clear gold that is the staple of my state.

Those trees are firmly rooted in place, where they have been for generations. People have come and gone, wars have been fought, tragedies overcome, but they still stand tall and unmoving.

Those trees are my teachers, my mentors, and the biggest life lessons I've ever learned were out there in the land that is one final payment away from being mine.

"Well, you sure clean up nicely, honey. Where are you off to tonight? Shall I ring ahead and tell them to warn the nice boys?" Mom says, running her hands down over my shoulders and pretending to straighten my sweater.

"Don't worry, Ma. I'm not looking for the nice boys." I wink and kiss her cheek.

She's still shaking her head when I disappear into the hallway to grab my shoes and leave.

I score a parking spot not far from Church Street, which is a win considering it's Friday, and while the freezing temperatures won't turn people away from Burlington's pedestrian-only social bubble, they definitely make people less keen on walking.

If you're looking for a nice, inclusive bar to hang out and score the occasional hookup, Vino and Veritas has your back. While it's not a gay bar, the rainbow flags in the window definitely attract the breath of the LGBT population in Burlington.

I spot Andy and Wyatt through the window as I cross the road. They've grabbed us a booth, and each has a drink, but Noah isn't there, so my first stop as soon as I enter the bar, through the common main entrance with the bookstore next door, is to join them.

"It's not cheating," Wyatt says as I shrug my heavy coat and tuck it in the corner of the long seat.

"It is if you get a hard-on," Andy says.

"Oh, come on, you sport wood watching the Bruisers play."

"And your point?"

"Just because you get hard doesn't mean your heart is in it. It's not cheating."

I listen to the guys go back and forth for a while. This is not a conversation I want to get involved in, even though I know they don't mean half of the stuff they tease each other about.

Andy and Wyatt used to be flatlanders, what we fondly call people who weren't raised here, but one look at them now—from their change in accent down to their clothes—you would think they're born and bred Vermonters.

They met on their first day of college at the University of Vermont when they realized they were roommates. Legend says they hooked up that day and haven't been apart since.

I can only imagine what it would be like to find your soulmate that easily, but it's not a thought I want to entertain. It's not something that will ever happen to me, so I focus on tonight.

With any luck, I'll find a guy to have some no-strings fun with, and the worst that can happen is that I'll have some fun trying.

Noah arrives ten minutes after me, bringing Andy and Wyatt's discussion to an end. It's been a while since we were all together, so I ask what everyone's been up to.

"Sorry I'm late, guys. I wanted to put Ollie to bed," Noah says.

He looks tired, but I've never seen him so happy.

"How's my little wingman?" I ask.

In our friend group, Noah and I are the ones who've known each other the longest. We went to the same high school and, while we weren't friends then, we got to know each other better when my brother dated his sister for a while.

Their relationship didn't last, but we became friends and have been ever since. I was the best man at his wedding to his high school sweetheart and, more recently, became a godparent to his almost one-year-old son, Oliver.

I'd never thought about having kids myself. I always figured it was something I'd decide when I was in a stable relationship, but the moment I met Oliver, it was love at first sight. The little man seems to like me, too, so here we are. I'm the proud example-setting grownup to the cutest kid in the world.

"He's teething, which means he's moodier than March in Vermont," he says.

"Maybe he just needs to spend a day with Uncle Skyler, check out some bars, hit on the pretty boys. You know, a regular Tuesday afternoon," I tease.

He snorts, but I'm not letting him destroy my plans to educate my cute sidekick in the ways of the world, so I stand up from the table.

"The usual?" I ask, pointing at the empty glasses.

"You know it," Andy says, and both Wyatt and Noah nod.

"If you've got your flirting game on, the new bartender is H.O.T.," Wyatt says.

I look at Andy, who nods. "He has this sexy kind of European vibe going on."

And now I know how their earlier conversation got started.

I scan the bar but don't see anyone I don't already know. Then again, it's pretty busy out there.

Someone steps away from the bar area with a tray of drinks, and I immediately take their place. All the bartenders are busy, so I look around to inspect this evening's crowd.

A glass breaks somewhere behind the bar, taking my attention from the crowd waiting to be served to the clumsy bartender on the far end from where I'm standing.

He must be the new guy because I know I'd recognize that ass if I'd seen it before. Scrap that. I'd have tapped it. My eyes scan the rest of him, taking the time to appreciate his slim body from behind.

His dark jeans hug his ass perfectly, and his thighs...damn, those thighs look strong and...*fuck.* My dick responds to the way he moves as he's crouching to pick up the glass from the floor.

The dark button-down shirt is loose on him, and I wonder if it's a standard V&V-issued shirt because a guy that wears *those* jeans wouldn't possibly choose to wear anything but a fitted shirt.

He washes his hands after disposing of the glass and then runs them through his dark-blond hair. I wonder if, in the light of day, his hair is actually a lighter shade.

Turn around, baby. Let me see your face.

And as if the god of horny gay single men is listening to my prayers, the guy turns around. He looks flustered and annoyed.

There's something about him I can't put my finger on, but it doesn't take me long to figure out what it is. Why he looks so familiar.

When he looks up, and his eyes meet mine, my body locks up in shock. I close my eyes and open them again because this isn't happening. I must be dreaming while awake.

I smile, wanting to jump over the counter to touch him. It's the only way to be sure, but he looks as though he's seen a ghost.

One of the other bartenders bumps against him, making him jolt and take a side step.

I smile at him, and that's when I see the very slight shake of his head as I call to him before he runs to the staff area behind the bar.

"Jud!"

③

JUDSON

Skyler fucking West. The one person I was hoping I wouldn't run into.

I brace myself against the kitchen sink.

The cook ignores me. I'm not his favorite person right now. It's only my second day, and I've already accidentally pissed him off by asking about his knife when I noticed the irregular size of his chopped onion.

Who knew he'd get so offended? I'm pretty sure he only needs to sharpen the knives, and it would make a hell of a difference. It's not like I was criticizing his knife skills. I mean, I could have, but I didn't.

The other bartenders walk past me, holding plates stacked with potato chips, maple pigs, and mixed olives.

It's a busy Friday night, and even if it's not the kind of busy I'm used to, I don't want to let my boss or my colleagues down.

My boss, Tanner, is a man of few words. Fortunately for me, that's a language I'm fluent in. Try working in the kitchen of a French restaurant, and you soon find out words are at a premium. Unless you manage to let the béarnaise sauce curdle right in the middle of a busy evening service. In that case, you find yourself questioning all of the life decisions that led you to be on the receiving end of the head chef's anger.

"Hey, you okay?" Molly asks. This is my first shift with her. She's nice, but I don't know how she got the job because she must be the worst bartender I've ever met.

Not that I'm one to talk when I've just broken a glass, not to mention my total lack of knowledge of the local craft beers and ales the bar serves.

I'm good with wine, though, which I guess is the reason Tanner hired me since that was the first question he asked me when I enquired about the part-time vacancy.

"Don't worry about the glass," Molly says when I don't reply. "I break one at least every few days, and that's when I don't drop a whole tray. I swear Rainn will kill me one day."

"Who?" I ask.

She waves her hand. "He's not in tonight, but you'll meet him soon."

"If I don't lose my job first." I laugh.

"Nah, you'd have to screw up more than I do, and that's very unlikely. Although you should probably get back out there. It's pretty busy."

She leaves me, and not a moment later, I hear the sound of broken glass followed by Molly apologizing.

It's like she tries so hard to be a better bartender, but everything around her conspires against it.

I heard someone say she's an amazing singer, so maybe we have a lot more in common than a tendency to break a glass.

We're both in jobs we're not suited to while our dreams are out there being crushed.

If she tells me she also has a dickhead ex, then I might just adopt her as my new best friend.

Speaking of which…

I take a deep, steady breath.

I need to go back to the bar before I get in trouble and not even all the wine knowledge I hold in my head will save me.

Straightening my black shirt, I raise my head and prepare to get back to work. Who knows, maybe this was all a figment of my imagination, and I didn't really see Skyler looking all tall and grownup on the other side of the bar.

It's not like I'd know what he looks like now, anyway. So it's probably—definitely—all in my head.

Then how did he know your name?

I tell my brain to shush and go back to the bar.

It's as busy as Molly says. Busier than it was before, so I approach a customer to take their order, totally avoiding looking in the direction I last saw the Skyler apparition.

"You might want to serve that dude over there," Molly says.

"Who?"

"The blond Henry Cavill in the corner. He's asked for you three times. Serve him so he can give up the space to a new customer."

I look over, and sure enough, Skyler's still there. He waves at me, and his smile throws me a little, but I have years of practice letting people see only what I want them to see.

"What can I get you, sir?" I take a wet cloth to wipe the bar and avoid making eye contact.

"Jud, it's me, Sky."

He puts his hand on mine, and I finally look up to meet his gaze. It's not fair how good he looks.

He still has that smile, with slightly longer canines and one tooth crooked enough to make his smile perfectly imperfect.

"My name is Judson. Can I get you something to drink or a snack? Would you like to see the menu?" I ask, pulling my hand back.

"Judson?" He laughs. "It was Jud for the first eighteen years of your life."

"Sixteen."

"What?"

"Sixteen, you didn't talk until you were two."

He crooked his head. "So you *do* remember me."

"Of course I do. I still need to take your order, or I'll need to serve someone else. It's quite busy." I hope he takes the message that I'm at work and can't talk.

"Four Shipley ciders."

Thankfully, he's asked for something I do know, so I won't make a joke of myself asking for help from one of the other bartenders.

I give him the bottles and wait for him to put the money on the bar. He drops a couple of bills, but when I go to take them, he holds onto them.

"When did you get back?" he asks.

"Why?" A different question is on the tip of my tongue, but I'm still not ready to process what's happening right now.

Skyler's brows furrow, and his smile dwindles. I feel bad for a hot second until I remember who he is and what he did.

"Because—"

He's interrupted by a guy who sidles up to him. "Dude, the troops are getting thirsty. Flirt all you want, but don't leave us dry."

Skyler says, "I wasn't." At the same time, I say, "What?"

The guy narrows his eyes, looking me up and down. "Oh fuck. He's not gay, is he? Damn shame." He shrugs before taking three ciders and leaving Skyler behind.

"I should probably…" He points to the table where his friend is sitting with two other guys.

I nod and go to the other side of the bar to serve customers.

What did the guy mean about flirting? Did he think I was flirting with Skyler? Like that would ever happen.

The rest of my shift goes smoothly and without any more breakages, but I feel Skyler's eyes on me all night.

I steal some glances, noticing that he's approached by a few different guys.

Skyler was always the popular kid, from kindergarten through to high school, and it looks like that hasn't changed one bit.

They sit and chat before leaving him and his friends. It's clear two of the guys are a couple, which explains why he's in this bar. I can't imagine Skyler would frequent a gay bar. Though Vino and Veritas isn't exactly a gay bar, more a welcoming space for the LGBTQ+ community.

For all of Skyler's flaws, homophobia was never one of them.

I know because I came out to him when I was twelve.

My mind takes me back to that time when I'd spent two weeks picking fights with him until our moms grounded us together and I came clean. I thought I was going to lose my best friend as soon as I told him I liked boys, so I'd decided that if we hated each other already, it would be easier.

Skyler simply said he didn't care that I was gay, but he was annoyed that we had to spend the afternoon indoors.

Tanner taps my shoulder and nods for me to follow him to the storage room.

This is it. The moment he decides that no amount of wine knowledge can make up for breaking a glass and pissing off the cook.

"Settling in okay?" he asks.

"Yeah, everyone's been great. I'm trying to memorize the drinks. I did break a glass, which I can pay for, of course..." *Shut up, Jud.*

Tanner seems to ignore my ramble because he picks up a box and takes it to a nearby table.

"We got these samples from a new supplier. I have no clue if they're good or not."

I look at the wine bottles and take one out of the box. It's a Guigal Côtes du Rhône, a red wine with bold flavors of dark fruits and a peppery note. The next one is a white wine produced at the Cave de Lugny.

Tanner stares at me, and I can't tell if he's about to fire me or if he's testing me. An idea builds in my head.

"These are good, inexpensive wines. If you want, I could do a wine tasting session for the bartenders and tell them more about the wines, especially why they're good choices when paired with some of the food we serve."

He grunts his reply, and I'm not sure if he likes the idea or not.

"Can you come in early on Wednesday?"

"Sure."

"Okay, thanks."

He closes the box and puts it back on a shelf.

"That's it? I'm not fired?" I ask.

"Should I?" He raises a brow.

I shake my head, and he leaves the storage room.

When I return to the bar, I no longer see Skyler or his friends.

A tiny pang of regret settles in my stomach until I quash it. I'm not the one who betrayed my best friend.

Cleaning the bar after we close feels surprisingly soothing. Someone picks a soft jazz playlist, and Molly sings along to it. She does have a beautiful, soulful voice. All the clumsiness and forgetfulness is nowhere while she's singing, and I wonder if she'd be a better bartender if she could sing while she's working.

The house is quiet when I get in. I grab a shower and go to bed, knowing I'll still be up early enough in the morning, thanks to my chef's body clock.

Maybe it's time to ask my mom some questions. Specific, Skyler-related questions.

She's been pressing for me to reach out to him. I won't tell her why I can't do that, but I can find out what's been happening while I was gone.

SKYLER

"Wanna talk about it?" Noah asks.

"About what?"

We're re-arranging the living room for Ollie's first birthday party, making space for people to sit and putting away anything that might be easily breakable.

Who knew you'd need the same level of care for the party of a one-year-old as you do for a twenty-year-old.

We should know. After all, we trashed Noah's place a few times before we decided to grow up. Well, *he* decided to grow up.

Fortunately, their house is huge, so there's plenty of space for people to move around.

"You were all pensive last week at Vino, and since then, you've been quiet. No calls, no messages."

"Shit, man, I'm sorry. I'll do better this week," I say.

"Dude, Ollie can live without his daily cow selfies. I just wondered what that was all about last weekend. When Wyatt came back with the drinks, he said there was this weird tension between you and the bartender."

I take a deep sigh.

"Do you remember Judson Hale?"

"Your best friend? The one who left?"

"Yeah."

Noah stares at me for a moment before the pieces slot into place. "That was him? The bartender? Wait...he's back? Did you know?"

"No." I run my hand over the back of my neck, poking my tired muscles. "I mean, yes, that was him, but no, I didn't know he was back."

"Wow. Are you going to speak to him? Find out why he was gone all this time?"

I push the couch so it's where Noah wants it and then sit on it, leaning forward with my forearms on my knees. "I don't know."

When I saw him, all the feelings I had ten years ago came rushing back, along with the confusion and betrayal. Why did he leave without saying a word?

I'm angry that, whatever happened, neither I nor our friendship meant enough to him for even a goodbye, a message, an email.

In the last ten years, I've relied on bites of second- and third-hand information.

After a while, I stopped tuning into conversations whenever his name was mentioned because it hurt too much to hear he was out there fulfilling our dream without me.

I don't want thoughts of Jud to ruin this day, so I stand up and move the other couch before declaring the room suitable to be trashed by a rowdy bunch of babies and toddlers.

"Babe, can you get Ollie? He just woke up," Anita shouts from the kitchen.

My eyes meet Noah, and we both smile and run up the stairs to Ollie's bedroom.

He's sitting in his crib, holding onto his favorite toy, a baby cow I gave him when he was born.

Ollie's squishable cheeks are pink from teething, but he's smiling, and as soon as he sees me, he waves his arms.

"Moo Moo."

I pick him up while Noah grabs the stuff we need to change him and get him dressed for the party.

"I'll let you off today because it's your birthday, but from tomorrow, I'm Uncle Sky or just Sky. I'll even take Dude, just *not* Moo Moo."

"Moo Moo," he says again, holding onto my shirt. I boop his nose and hold him close, inhaling his baby scent. God, I love how he smells.

Anita keeps teasing, saying I'm broody, but I don't think I'm ready for children just yet. Where would I even find the time? It doesn't stop me from loving this particular tiny human though.

When Ollie is dressed, we take a selfie before going downstairs. We look so cool with our matching sweaters that say Birthday Dude, Daddy Dude, and Moo Dude.

Okay, so maybe I'm enabling the nickname a little.

We put on our best smiles and go in the kitchen to show off our party outfits.

I hear voices and some laughter as we approach.

"If you want, I can send you the recip—" Jud stops when he looks up and sees me.

"Oh my gosh, don't all you look adorable," Anita says. I'm holding Ollie, who now wants his mommy. Anita takes him, giving him a kiss and straightening his sweater. "Skyler, I'm going to take back your Ollie cuddle privileges. Why didn't you tell me Judson is back in town?"

I do a doubletake before remembering that Anita was in our senior class.

Jud stares at me and then at Anita.

"Um…that's actually my fault. I didn't want to make a big deal of it, so I asked him not to tell anyone." He smiles and points to the door. "I'll just go back out to get your cupcakes, and then I'll be out of your hair. I'm sure you have a lot of stuff to do."

When he leaves, both Anita and Noah stare at me, and I can tell by their faces it's for very different reasons.

"Maybe I should see if he needs help."

I find Jud staring at the back of a van. When he sees me, he opens the door and starts stacking the cupcake boxes.

"Do you need help?" I ask.

"No, thanks." He grabs the boxes and uses his foot to close the van door, walking around me to go inside the house.

I stare at him from behind. He walks with confidence now. He's lost weight, and his clothes fit him perfectly, but there's...something else different about him.

He comes out of the house, holding the keys to the van in his hand, and stops when he sees I haven't moved.

We're only a few feet away from each other, and I take a moment to really look at him.

Big blue eyes, a small round nose, the same freckles, and the beauty spot under his right eye. I don't need to be closer to know that I'm staring at my old best friend.

Except we're anything but best friends now. He's a stranger who looks like someone who knows how to stand up for himself. I don't know if the thought makes me proud of him or sad that I would no longer be his protector.

I don't know what he sees as he stares back at me. Does he see the friend with whom he spent countless nights, looking at photos of places around the world under a bedsheet, pretending it was a travel machine? Does he see the friend who would sneak in maple candy for him in his school bag and forget about it until ants were crawling all over his books?

Or does he see...me?

"Did you want anything?" he asks.

"Are you staying?"

"Today or forever?"

"Both?

"No."

I nod. "It's nice to see you back...for as long as you are here. Your parents must be so happy."

"I didn't think you'd still be here," he says before he closes his mouth as if he wasn't expecting to catch himself talking.

His comment taps into a part of my past that I took a long time to heal from. But that's ancient history now. I smile and mean it. "There are a lot of really good reasons to stay."

Jud points at the house.

"Among other things. Noah and Anita are good friends... maybe..." Should I say it? Fuck it. "Maybe we can...I don't know, meet up some time to talk?"

He pulls his sweater down, and a warm feeling spreads through me. That was such a Jud thing when he was feeling self-conscious about his weight.

This Jud doesn't seem to lack self-confidence, so maybe the gesture is so ingrained in him that he doesn't even notice when he does it.

"I don't think that's a good idea."

"Why?"

"Because we're different people. We grew up. There's no reason to assume we'd still be friends."

"And whose fault is that, huh?" I'm unable to keep the edge off my voice.

He looks around us, and I notice some guests arriving.

"We can talk about whose fault it is, or we can pretend we haven't seen each other."

I take a step closer but then hear someone call my name. I groan when I see who it is.

Jeff approaches, giving me a kiss on the cheek.

"Hey, babe," he says, placing a claiming hand on my lower back. I step away from him.

"Hi. What are you doing here?" I ask.

"My nephew isn't feeling well, so I've been tasked with bringing the gift to the birthday boy...hey, once I've done this, do you want to—?"

"No," I say, knowing how abruptly that came out. "Sorry. I mean, I can't. Ollie's my godson. I'm not leaving his party."

Jeff shrugs. "Too bad. See you soon...you know you'll want to." He winks and then jogs to the door.

When I look back at Jud, he's staring with his mouth wide open.

"What?"

"You want to know why we can't be friends? Why we can't pick up where we left off, Skyler? Because you were in my life for eighteen years. Eighteen fucking years and I feel like I never truly knew you. That," he points to the door where Jeff is talking to Anita, "just proves it."

He starts walking toward the van. I follow and grab his arm, forcing him to turn around to face me.

"What do you mean?" I ask.

"You're gay or bi? Because last time I checked, you were straight, but I don't believe for a second that wasn't the setup for a rendezvous."

I can't keep from laughing. "Rendezvous? On this side of the ocean, we call it a hookup. Wait...how do you not know I'm gay?"

"You're gay?" His voice goes up a notch at the same time that he checks me out from head to toe. Is that a French thing? Are the French so open-minded about sex that they're able to freak out and assess a potential sexual partner at the same time?"

The thought makes me laugh even harder.

"What's so funny?"

"You, Judbug. How did you not know I'm gay?"

"Very easily. I haven't seen you for nine years, seven months, and three days. I've gotta go."

He leaves me on the sidewalk, staring at the back of his van with jumbled thoughts, jumbled feelings, and maybe a little bit of hope.

The only thing is, I don't have a clue what I'm hoping for.

5

JUDSON

I open my closet and take out one of my new work shirts. This one fits better than the one I found at the back of the closet last week. It's suitable enough for work, but it doesn't fit properly, and I don't like how it makes me feel.

Ill-fitting. Not quite good enough.

Or maybe it has nothing to do with the shirt and everything to do with bumping into Skyler twice within a week.

I need to remember this town isn't that big, and now, I don't have the anonymity of the big metropolitan city. People here still remember me.

Or better, they remember the chubby gay kid with the awkward thick-rimmed glasses always falling down his face.

Not that I still wear glasses. Laser eye surgery took care of that a few years ago.

And I'm no longer chubby. Hearing people call me the fat, lazy American chef behind my back, and sometimes to my face, hurt at first, until I proved them wrong by losing the weight and becoming the youngest sous chef to work in one of Paris's most prestigious restaurants.

I button up the shirt, wondering what Skyler thinks of how I look now.

At least, unlike the first time I'd seen him, the second time I'd been wearing clothes that actually fit me. Who knew that helping my mom out by making the birthday cake and cupcake delivery for her would put me face to face with him again.

Dammit, I promised myself I wasn't going to think about him. Stupid brain.

The conversation we had outside Noah and Anita's place has been on a loop inside my head like one of those songs you can't stop singing.

Skyler is gay. I let that sink in...because it seems that days of thinking about it haven't done the job.

I know that every person comes out in their own time, but how did I not even have a clue? It's not like he was actively chasing girls in high school, but he did have a couple of girl-friends, and he never mentioned boys in any way.

Did he wait until I was gone to come out? No, that doesn't make sense because even I hadn't known I was going to leave when I did.

I brush my thoughts aside. I especially don't want to think about how he's only gotten better looking since we were eighteen.

He's taller and more muscular than I thought possible. When Molly referred to him as the Henry Cavill look alike, she wasn't wrong.

Skyler looks like he could throw me around and do what he wants with...wait...what?

I shake my thoughts away again and grab my wallet and phone.

Today, I'm doing the wine tasting for the bartenders, so I need to get to Vino earlier, which also has the silver lining of missing dinner at home. I don't want to break my mom's heart, but I can't continue to eat so much food.

I'm taking my chicken salad from the fridge when the door to the backyard opens.

There's a gasp as I close the fridge door, and I realize it's not my mom coming back in but Skyler's mom.

Mrs. West and my mom met at the maternity ward when Skyler and I were born only hours apart, and they've been friends ever since.

She rushes over to put her arms around me, squeezing tight.

"Oh my goodness, sweetheart. It's so nice to see you." She pulls back, looking me up and down. "You look great, Judson. You lost weight though. Are you eating enough?"

"He is, but then he goes on his long runs every morning and loses it all again," my mom says, coming into the kitchen.

"Hi, Mrs. West. It's nice to see you too." I turn to my mom. "And I need to run because if I don't, I won't fit in any of my clothes by next week."

My mom raises her hands. "Shoot a woman for wanting to cook for her son when he returns home after ten years."

I pull her in for a hug. "Thank you for all your wonderful food, Mom."

"I don't think Skyler could survive away from my cooking very long. He sure does put away all the food he can get his hands on. Then again, he needs it..." she pauses, and her smile leaves her for a moment. "He works so hard. Sometimes I wish he didn't have to...anyway... How are you? Are you back to stay?"

"I'm not sure," I say, and then look at my mom, who's now lost her smile.

In the same way that we haven't talked about why I'm back home, we also haven't talked about my plans. And that's because I don't have any.

For the first time in my life, I want to make a decision that isn't fueled by how someone makes me feel. I don't want to do it out of hurt or spite. I want to do it for me because it's the right thing.

"I've gotta go."

"So early?" my mom asks.

"Yeah, I'm giving a wine-tasting class." The thought gives me a rush of energy. I always get a kick out of sharing my knowledge and seeing people learn and improve. Since I'm not in a kitchen anymore, this is the next best thing.

I give my mom a kiss and grab my salad box.

"See you in the morning, Mom. Nice to see you again, Mrs. W."

Renting a car is a necessity that I resent. I'd happily walk to work, but late at night when I'm at the bar until we close, it's not as nice walking back home in the freezing-cold darkness.

I find a parking spot a couple of blocks away from Church Street.

Tanner lets me in through the loading bay door since the bar is still closed. I'm earlier than everyone else, so I can set up.

"I put a few tables together, and there's a tray with clean glasses out there," Tanner says. "I'm going to run over to The Maple Factory to grab a couple of boxes of crullers. I can't have half-drunk bartenders, even if it is a quiet weekday."

I laugh and realize those are the most words I've heard Tanner say. "I'm sure they'll appreciate it, but they'll be tasting the wine, not drinking it."

He raises a brow that tells me maybe fifty percent of the wine will not be spit back into the glasses.

I start by opening the bottles of red to let them breathe and then arranging my display first by region and then in the order they'll be tasting them.

Thirty minutes later, I feel nervousness settling in, but also excitement that I get to talk about one of my favorite topics. I'd give anything to talk about food or do a cooking demonstration, but sometimes you take what you're given.

"Unlike foreign wines, which are labeled according to the grape used, French wines are labeled according to the soil on which they were produced," I say, pointing to the different groupings of bottles.

"I thought it was all about the grapes," Rainn says.

"The orientation of a vineyard toward the sun, the humidity of the region, and temperature variations are what alter the flavor of the wine. If you plant the same variety of grape in different regions, you end up with different tasting wines. The type of grape is only one of the factors that determine the taste, acidity, and even alcohol level of the wine."

We have limited time, so after my introduction, we get to the tasting part. I love watching everyone's face as they taste the wines and try to determine the flavors that come through on their palate.

Surprisingly, there's very little actual drinking. I suspect it would be a different outcome if we were tasting cider or ale.

When we're done, everyone helps clean up, clearing the mess in no time with the promise of free crullers.

I pass on the crullers, but I should eat something before my shift, so I grab my salad from the staff refrigerator.

"Thank you for that session. It was really informative," Tanner says.

"Thank you. You have no idea how much I needed this." I scratch the back of my neck. "It may not surprise you, but as a chef, tending bar isn't…the same."

He taps my shoulder. "Sometimes an unexpected change is the shortcut to finding what you need." He has the night off, so he leaves me to think about his parting words before going upstairs to the place he shares with his boyfriend, Jax.

Rainn told me that before meeting Tanner, Jax had been in the hostel across the road when it caught fire and had lost all of his belongings.

I finish my salad and get ready to work. My chef's brain has memorized all the drinks we sell, so as long as no one asks for my opinion and just tells me what they want, I'm good.

Thoughts of Skyler leave me blissfully alone until I overhear a conversation from a group that's sitting at the table closest to the bar. It's quiet enough in the bar that I can make out what they're saying.

"Stop talking about pancakes. I ran out of maple syrup, and Skyler won't be at the farmer's market this week," one girl says. "Don't even get me started on the maple cream. I'm down to my last quarter of a jar. Death is impending."

"Why not?" another one asks.

"It's tapping season."

The group all nod and take a sip of their drinks, seemingly satisfied with the answer, but now I'm the one with the questions.

What did they mean about it being tapping season? How is that related to Skyler?

I suddenly realize how little I know about him. I don't know if he went to college or if he went traveling like he wanted to.

I assume that since he's still around, he's working on his family's farm, which doesn't make sense because that was always Miles's dream.

Skyler wanted to see the world before doing his business degree. We were going to open a restaurant together.

"Hey, you okay? You've been cleaning the same spot for god knows how long," Molly says.

"Yeah, sorry, just lost in thought."

She nods. "Happens to me a lot too."

I spot a customer approaching the bar. "Let me get this guy, and then I'll tell you all about Paris."

The light in her eyes brings me completely back to the present, where I work at a bar with cool people.

My mom is sitting at the kitchen table with her old recipe book when I get home from the bar.

"Hey, honey, how was work?" she asks.

"It was good. I did a wine-tasting session for the guys."

She nods.

I sit next to her, wondering how I can broach the topic I've been thinking about since I first ran into Skyler.

"Mom...I...um, can I ask you about Skyler?"

She stares at me open-mouthed, which is understandable. She'd been complicit in my escape to Europe, even though she'd tried her best to convince me to talk to Skyler. I never told her what happened, but when I asked her to trust my judgment, she did so without reservation. I also told her I never wanted to hear his name again.

"You know I'm not the person you should be talking to, Judson."

I know that, but I'm too chicken-shit to speak to Skyler and, at the same time, too curious to not ask about him.

She closes her recipe book and holds her hands together. "Skyler is a good, hard-working man. It's thanks to him that his family still has a roof over their heads. I'm telling you this because I think you need to know that he hasn't had it easy since you left. Go talk to him."

Go talk to him.

As if it's that easy. I may have moved on, but I haven't forgotten, and I'm not sure I've forgiven.

6

SKYLER

I lay the flowers on the ground and then remove my gloves to touch the gravestone.

"Thank you, Albert. It's going to be another great season. Keep looking after our trees." I put my gloves back on.

The maple tree next to Albert's grave is the only one in this part of the forest that isn't tapped. It's Albert's, and it always feels like he's alive in the forest through that tree. It would be wrong to tap it.

I take a deep breath, closing my eyes and inhaling the scent of the forest.

This is my favorite time of the year. There's a fresh layer of snow on the ground that has already covered any evidence that I was here yesterday.

It's cold enough to freeze my balls, but when I'm here, this is the most peaceful I ever feel.

This forest is where my dreams come true, where my hard work produces something I'm proud of, something no one can take away from me.

I grew up idolizing my dad, hearing him say the farm belonged to the family, but he was the boss, so whatever he said was to be believed, trusted, and obeyed.

When I was nineteen, he showed my family exactly how little his word is worth, and I vowed to myself that whatever I ended up doing, I wouldn't be like him.

Whatever promises I make to this forest, I keep them all.

The forest is my stronghold, to be cherished and protected, and in it, I'm the boss.

Well, a boss freezing his balls off, but a boss, nonetheless.

I chuckle to myself and get back on the small tractor I rent just for the season. I've already done six trips to collect sap from the trees that aren't connected to the mainline that runs from most of the maple trees directly into the sugar house.

It's a complex network of pipelines that make collecting the sap a thousand times easier.

Unfortunately, it's also costly, which is the reason I don't have pipelines reaching the whole forest. As soon as my loan is paid off, I'll be looking into doing that.

This is my last trip for today. The sap collected via the mainline into the sap tank has been in the evaporator since before the sun was even up, and now I can add my manual collection.

By tomorrow morning, I should be able to filter the first syrup batch of the season, and as soon as I have enough syrup, I'll be making maple cream.

Maple cream is hard work to produce in any quantity, but I sell as much of it as I do the syrup, so it's worth the additional work.

I unload the tractor and then park it next to the sugar house. I don't have a barn, so I cover it up with a thick tarp. It's not ideal, but maybe when Miles is back, he can help me build a small barn.

Now that Noah has Ollie, I feel bad asking him to give up his free time to build stuff with me.

That reminds me…

I pull out my phone and take a selfie with the trees and snow in the background and send it to Noah. My little man has gotten used to receiving a selfie from me every day, and I don't want to let him down.

Usually, I take it at the farm, where I grab whatever animal is close enough to feature in the photo, but this month it's going to be my ugly face and some pretty trees.

Even though the cabin is a hundred yards from the sugar house, I hear the sound of a car engine, even over the whirring of the reverse osmosis system.

I'm nowhere near the main road, so I make my way to the cabin, readying myself to send away whatever unwelcome visitor I have.

I take the steps up to the porch that wraps around the cabin and walk slowly to see who it might be before I'm seen.

A car I don't recognize is parked next to my truck, but there's no one inside.

It's been a long time since I've had investors trying to buy the land from me, but there's always someone who thinks they can do better than the ones before. Tempt me with more money.

I pick up the pace, making sure my visitor can hear me coming as I walk around the porch.

"I'm not selling—" I stop when I see Jud standing in front of the dooryard.

He takes a step backward and stares at me. He's wearing a bright-red winter jacket, red gloves, and a toque.

I try to ignore the longing in my chest when he looks so much like my old friend. The toque covering his hair brings out his blue eyes.

"Hi," he says.

"Hi...um, what are you doing here?"

"I wanted to apologize for being so..." He stops as if trying to think of the right word to say, so I volunteer it for him.

"Angry?"

"Um..."

"Why are you so angry with me? You were the one who left? You were there right next to me all of our life. We had plans and dreams, things we wanted to do together. And then you were gone." I try to leave out the hurt, but it's impossible because I've been waiting for answers for ten years.

"I'm not angry with you." He lets out an almost defeated sigh.

"Really? You could have fooled me."

"My mom told me I should come here and talk to you."

"Oh really? Well, you can tell your mom there are no hard feelings. You came, and now you can go. See you around, Judson."

Turning on my heels, I follow the porch around the house to the back, feeling all the anger I managed to suppress years ago.

I stare at the maple trees and appreciate their beauty, breathing in the cold air. I should take a break before I go back to the sugar house.

"I'm sorry. Please let me explain."

Jud has always been stubborn, so I'm not entirely surprised he didn't go when I asked him to.

"Fine," I say, but I take a stand by looking at my trees rather than at him.

There's a moment of silence. I know he's not gone because I would have heard the steps on the old wooden porch.

"Over the last ten years, I...um...I've avoided talking about you."

I can't help the hurt I feel as he says the words, but I try to put it aside to listen.

He continues, "I wasn't expecting to see you at the bar...I wasn't ready, and I know I was rude."

I hear more footsteps, and when he talks, I know he's closer. "I asked my mom what you've been doing all these years. She told me to come here to find my answers."

I'm not sure if I should feel happy that he's willing to talk now or if I should be angry that he wants answers from me when he is the one who left.

"Why?" I ask.

"Why what?"

"Why are you back?"

I look at him. He's still a few inches shorter than me, but now I'm bigger. I outweigh him by at least forty pounds, easily.

He looks down and takes his gloves off, running his hand

through the soft snow settled on the handrail that follows the porch around the cabin.

"I lost everything in Paris. My career, my relationship, my dignity, and my self-respect. I have...nothing." His voice breaks as if he's close to tears.

"Oh, for fuck's sake." It shouldn't surprise me that my first instinct is to break the distance between us and hug him. We're both wearing several layers of clothing, but I can still feel how warm he is, and that makes me happy.

My mom told me once that I've been protecting Jud since we were old enough to play with other kids. I once pushed a kid that took Jud's toy while we were at the playground. And it didn't stop there. As we went through school together, I was never very good at keeping my cool whenever anyone so much as looked at him wrong.

He hugs me tight before he pulls back, and I don't know what I see in his face, but the overwhelming feeling of wanting to make it better takes over.

"Come on. Let's have a warm drink inside. I'm quite attached to my balls and, at the moment, they feel like they could fall off from the cold."

Jud snorts and follows me.

He stops as soon as we're inside, his mouth falling open. "What is this place?"

I look around to see what he sees, and I feel nothing but pride.

So many hours spent ripping out fixtures, building new ones with Noah, and even bribing my brother with maple syrup in exchange for his help when he was home from college.

The cabin is a lot more modern on the inside than it looks on the outside.

"This is my place. I bought it and the forest six years ago after the old owner, Albert, died. I've spent a lot of time refurbishing it with Noah and Miles." I fill the coffee machine with water and grab two mugs from the cabinet.

Jud walks around the kitchen island, running his hand over the stone worktop.

"It's beautiful. The outside definitely doesn't give away what's inside."

I smile and then realize I have no clue if Jud drinks coffee, tea, or anything else.

"You drink coffee?"

"Yeah, black, no sugar," he says.

"The setup is intentional. The cabin belongs in the forest. When I'm outside sitting on the porch and looking out at the trees, I want to feel connected with nature, but when I'm inside, I want to feel connected with me."

"And that means a super-high-tech kitchen with two ovens, a stovetop, a big fridge..."

I laugh and shrug. "I can't cook to save my life, but I guess I hoped one day I'd be with someone who'd appreciate the modern fixtures."

"So you live here? What about the farm?"

I fill the mugs with coffee and bring them to the island, where Jud takes a seat on one of the stools.

"I live here part-time. I still work on the farm...well, at least until Miles comes back from college and takes over the business. It's not a drive I want to do every day, so I stay mostly with my parents unless I need time for myself or I'm working here."

Jud takes a sip of his coffee, staring at it for a moment.

"I'm sorry I left."

7

JUDSON

Skyler stares at me as if he wants to look deep into my mind to find answers, but he's also afraid of what he'll see there.

I don't know if I can give him the answers he wants. I don't know if I have them myself.

I don't even know why I said what I said.

Maybe it's because my head is all jumbled up.

Even though I didn't tell him what happened in Paris, just saying *something* happened was enough to bring it all back, and then his hug...

Fuck. His hug was everything I didn't know I needed.

I jump a little on the stool when Skyler holds out his hand toward me.

"Hi, I'm Skyler."

I look at it and then at him. He's smiling, but his forehead is crinkled into a couple of lines.

Is this what he wants? A fresh start?

Recently, I've been wondering if there's more to what happened ten years ago. After all, Skyler seems hurt that I left. I'm not sure I'm ready to face that particular memory, but I think I'd like to meet the adult version of my friend.

"Hello," I say, shaking his hand. "I'm Judson."

"Nice to meet you. Can I call you Jud? You look like a Jud."

I narrow my eyes, and he laughs.

"Okay, so maybe we're not there yet."

"Tell me about the place. You said you work here. What do you do? Other than exquisite interior design, of course," I ask.

Skyler smiles. "Of course. I do have good taste for a late-blooming gay."

I snort and nearly spit my coffee. "When did you come…sorry, that's probably not…sorry."

"How about we do the now stuff, and when we're both ready, we do the before stuff?"

I nod my agreement, and then laughter I can't hold in bubbles out of me.

"Sorry," I say. "It's just that, considering everything, we're being such adults. When the fuck did we grow up?"

Skyler's smile leaves him, and I wonder what it was I said to make that happen.

"First year of college. Christmas break."

I stare at him. So he did go to college.

"That's when I grew up," he says.

"We don't have to talk about it. We decided on leaving the past for now."

"Have you finished your coffee?" he asks.

I give him my empty mug, and he puts both of them in the sink.

"Come on. Let's go for a walk outside."

I follow his lead, putting on my coat, gloves, and toque.

The snow is crunchy under my feet. I have a sudden desire to grab a handful and throw it at Skyler.

He's a few feet ahead of me and keeps looking back. I don't know if he's onto me or if he's afraid that I won't be here anymore if he stops watching.

We head into the forest, which is mostly just made of maple trees. There's no other vegetation around, and I wonder if he cleans the forest ground. I almost laugh at myself for having the thought.

Why on earth would anyone do that?

"My dad has a gambling problem."

I almost bump into Skyler's back when I don't realize he stopped.

"What?"

"The summer we graduated high school, some of the cows got sick. The milk production slowed, and we didn't realize the cows were sick until it was too late. We ended up losing a few cows. The financial impact was devastating, but my dad was always upbeat and kept saying we'd be fine."

Skyler starts walking again. I keep up the pace right beside him.

"For a while, we were able to cover some bills and the costs of running the farm. Mom took over part of the land to grow vegetables for her pickles and chutneys. She started selling them at the farmer's market on Church Street. We thought we'd get through it, and then after the winter, we'd buy new cows and restart production."

He sighs. "Long story short, my dad is a gambling addict who got us into more debt trying to win money to save the business. The whole thing nearly broke us. In the end, he agreed to speak to a therapist about his addiction and let me take over the accounts for the business. I had no clue what I was doing…"

"And that's when you grew up," I finish for him.

"Yeah."

"I'm really sorry, Skyler. I know you had so many dreams," I say.

Skyler's eyes are piercing as he stares at me.

"How about you? You said you lost everything," he prompts.

"It's a lame story. How about this? I went to one of the toughest culinary schools in the world, but no one took me seriously because I was the fat, lazy American," I say, raising my hands to do the quote sign with my fingers. "Yup, Europeans think very highly of us. To be fair, I *was* fat, so they weren't entirely wrong."

"Jud—"

"Nope, no interruptions, this is my turn. So anyway. I developed a crush on this guy in my class, Pierre. He's half-British, half-French. The perfect mix of self-deprecating and arrogant. Deadly."

Skyler chuckles.

"It took me a year to lose my weight and feel comfortable enough to buy new clothes and find a little bit of confidence. He noticed and asked me out. Fast forward five years, and we open a restaurant together in one of Paris's upcoming areas. Upcoming enough that we got a lot of attention, but not upcoming enough that we couldn't afford the rent if you know what I mean."

"You have a restaurant?" Skyler asks.

"Had."

"Sorry."

I shrug. "Last month we had a particularly busy time, which also coincided with a change of the menu. I always put in more hours because I liked to research local suppliers and put together interesting and innovative menus."

"It must have been stressful," he says.

"It was, but I loved it. Anyway, Pierre insisted we needed at least one night off to rest, but since the restaurant was busy, we took it in turns. He ended up catching a cold and stayed home a few extra nights.

"I don't like where this is going," Skyler says.

I purse my lips and nod. "One night, we had a particularly slow evening, so I decided to go home to keep him company. I worked most of the night, but as soon as I felt it was safe to go, I went home. I caught him in our bed with the sous chef who was also off that night because I was working."

"Fuck."

"I went to stay with a friend, but working alongside Pierre was a nightmare. After being caught, he was shameless about flirting with the other guy in front of everyone. It was embarrassing."

"Why didn't you leave?"

"Pierre's family has money, and they helped us get the restaurant started. I invested my savings into the restaurant. I couldn't just leave."

Skyler frowned as if to say, *but you're here now.*

"We were visited by a food critic. He's one of the most respected food critics because no one knows what he looks like. He picks random restaurants and dines like any other person. There's no way to prepare for his visit, so we had to be on point all the time." Well, there were ways to find out, but I'd been tired and distracted. "One of the kitchen assistants saw the review from the critic. It was the kind of review that can destroy someone's career. I don't know when he visited the restaurant. If I was cooking or if it was the night I left early, but it doesn't matter. I was the head chef. It was my kitchen. Pierre blamed me for everything. He said our reputation was ruined. No one would ever want to dine with us."

Skyler's laugh makes me look at him. "That's a bit dramatic, isn't it?"

"That's Paris for you. I wish I could shrug it off, but I've seen many chefs become unemployable because of some critics."

"And that's why you came back?"

"Yeah. So now I don't have a career, and my money is stuck in France. And while Pierre has agreed to buy me out, he's making it really difficult and blaming bureaucracy for not getting it done."

"Wow. That really sucks."

"Yeah, I guess neither of us has had it easy. And so much for not talking about the past," I joke.

He smiles. "Come on, let me show you something."

I follow him inside a big building that looks like a barn on the outside, but when we step inside, it's all shiny machinery and... that smell.

"Is that maple syrup?"

Skyler grins. "Not just any maple syrup. It's *the* best maple syrup you'll ever taste."

I see a shelf stocked with bottles. "Wait…that's the maple syrup my mom has at home. Maple Sky…fuck me…you *own* Maple Sky?"

He shrugs, and I laugh. "You better give me one of those bottles because I've just told you my sad loser story."

He hands me the bottle. "You're not a loser, Judson."

We talk more about his sugar-making business and the awards he's won. He asks me about Europe and how different it is from the States.

When I get in the rental to drive back home with my bottle of Maple Sky, I feel lighter than I've felt in a long time. Maybe even since I left Vermont.

Crazy, huh?

8

SKYLER

It's open mic night at Vino, so the bar is filling up already, even though it's too early.

Yep, you know you've reached higher levels of adulting when your group of friends time the outing to catch the first singer and then go home nice and early because it's a school night.

I slide into the booth next to Wyatt and Andy. Noah and Anita are both out with us today, which is a small miracle because they're still struggling to leave Ollie with Anita's parents.

They're lovely people, but I get it. I find it hard to say goodbye to Mr. Cuteface, and I'm not even his parent.

"You look like shit, man," Andy says.

"Thanks. Just what a girl wants to hear after changing her outfit five times," I say with a hint of humor. Just a hint because I don't think I have the energy for more.

I'm fucking exhausted.

"No, seriously. Are you okay?" Noah asks, and I see his face is laced with guilt.

In the last few years, as Maple Sky has gotten off the ground, Noah has been there for me, helping me increase the number of taps before I was able to install the tubing system. He was right there collecting gallons of sap from my maple trees into large vats that we carried all the way back to the sugar house.

More recently, he helped me with the setup of the sugar house. He knows it can be a one-man job most of the year, but I always need more help during tapping season.

This year, with having Ollie and getting a job promotion, he can't help me.

I understand it, and I wouldn't have it any other way. Besides, this might be the last year I'm doing it all on my own. That's what I hope, at least.

With my loan paid off, I'll be able to afford to expand the tubing system and hire someone to help me next year.

"I'm good. Just fucking exhausted. I need sleep more than I need my next meal."

"Those are two of the four great life necessities. We can help you with the third, but you're on your own for the fourth," Wyatt says.

"The fuck is he talking about? Andy, can you translate?"

Andy lines up the four empty bottles of cider they've already drunk.

"Food, drink, sleep, and sex." He gives Wyatt a heated look and then reorders the bottles.

I'm not sure what difference it makes since they're all the same, but I'm too tired to argue.

"Normally, you start with food and drink, and I can't stress the food part enough because if you have too much of the drink part first, then other parts of you stop working, and then that's just a sad day for all concerned."

Anita laughs, and Noah gives her an indignant stare.

"I hear you, girl," Andy says. "Once you're all set with food and drink, next comes sex and sleep."

Wyatt nods. "That right there is the key to happiness."

Noah slides out of the booth. "My turn to make you happy. Another round?"

Everyone cheers, and he makes his way around the tables to

the bar.

I see the regular bartenders but not Judson. When the guys called me to come out, I wondered if he'd be working tonight.

It's been almost three weeks since he turned up at the cabin and almost three weeks since I've seen him. I'm starting to wonder if I imagined it.

I don't think I did because I still have the mug he used sitting on my kitchen counter. I washed it, of course, but I couldn't put it back in the cabinet. It was a reminder that he'd been there and maybe that we can navigate this weird situation together.

He joked about the situation with his ex, but even after ten years, I can still see through Jud as clearly as I can the sap that seeps out of my maple trees.

If we can be friends, maybe... Fuck, I don't even know what that would mean.

"Did you see that?" Anita says.

I glance at her, and she's looking in my direction.

"What?" I peek behind me but don't see anything worthy of my attention.

"Yeah, I saw it," Andy says.

"Saw what?" Noah asks, coming back from the bar with his hands full of ice-cold Shipley cider.

"Skyler had a smile." Anita's eyes narrow as she leans forward to stare at me.

I laugh. "When have you ever seen me without a smile?" And it's true. Despite my life turning out differently from how I planned, I'm pretty happy.

I have more work than I can handle, but that's better than not having any work. I can smell my freedom from my family's business with each day that passes. Especially since Miles called me last week to say he may get home sooner than we expected.

"Not that kind of smile," she says.

I grab one of the drinks and take a swig.

"True. That was one up from your prowling smile," Andy says.

I coughed. "My prowling smile?"

"For such a big dude, you have smooth ninja moves when it comes to picking up guys. Don't think I haven't noticed. Only you can hold a conversation with us while also picking up someone to go home with, using a clever look and well-timed smile."

"Hey, I can't help it if I'm buff and adorable." I shrug. "I'm basically a puppy. You can't resist me."

They laugh, and Wyatt says, "Well, we're immune...but I have a feeling the new bartender in town is struggling."

"What?" I look toward the bar and see Jud. When our eyes meet, he smiles and waves.

I wave back.

"And there it is again, folks," Andy says, pretending to hold up a banner. "The smile. Trademark."

"Whatever you're thinking, I can assure you, you're wrong," I say, but I'm not sure there's any weight to my words.

The first singer comes on stage, and the buzz of conversation comes to a halt. It's Molly, one of the bartenders. She's a total disaster behind the bar, but when the girl opens her mouth, it's like the portal to a new, better world opens around us and we can walk in for free for as long as she's singing.

While everyone's distracted looking at the stage, I take a peek toward the bar again.

Judson is smiling at whoever he's serving, and it makes such a difference from the serious, grumpy man I met weeks ago. He looks more relaxed and sure of himself.

When he finishes with the bottle of scotch he's pouring, he reaches up to the shelf behind the bar. It's then that I notice he has the sleeves of his shirt rolled up and his arm is covered in tattoos.

My dick twitches in my jeans. Jud has tattoos? Is it just his arms? Does he have them anywhere else...everywhere else?

Fuck, I need to stop thinking about it before I get a full-on erection.

Our eyes meet again, and he stops for a second before smiling.

I'm moving out of the booth toward the bar before I can stop myself.

As if he knows I'm heading for him, he goes to the corner of the bar furthest from the stage.

"Hey," he says. "Can I get you a drink?"

"Hey. Shipley, please."

He grabs the bottle, twisting off the cap for me.

"How's work?" he asks.

"Busy. I can't remember the last time I slept."

"Is it always like that?"

I laugh. "Hell no. Maple tapping is a very short season. According to the weather forecast, I should have another two weeks to go, which works out perfectly."

"Why's that?"

"The Maple Festival in Fairlington."

Jud's eyes bulge out and his smile is wide. He places an arm on the bar, and I can't help look down at his tattoos. "Oh my god, I haven't been to the festival in…" he trails off.

"Ten years?" I add, but my eyes don't meet his. I'm still captivated by the colorful ink on his skin.

"Yeah…"

His voice is deeper, and when I look up, I'm met with the intensity of his blue eyes.

"You should go to the festival. I'm going to be there," I say.

"You are?"

"Yeah, I sell Maple Sky syrup and cream. You should go. It's basically chef porn on steroids for three days."

He scrunches his nose. "I'm not sure porn and steroids are my thing."

"Porn isn't your thing?" I tease, and my dick stands to attention at the sight of his flushed skin.

Once again, I find myself wondering the extent of Jud's tattoos and if they do a good job of hiding that blush.

He tilts his head and licks his lips. "I can do porn, and I can do maple syrup. I might check out the festival. Thanks for the heads-up." He winks and goes to the other side of the bar, where someone called him.

Abort. Abort.

I walk back to the table, trying to figure out how we went from barely speaking a word to each other to flirting in zero-point-three seconds.

My phone buzzes in my pocket, and I see I missed a call from my mom.

Ignoring the looks the guys and Anita are giving me, I say my goodbyes and leave.

I call my mom on my way to the truck.

"Hey, Ma, everything okay?"

"I'm sorry to bother you, honey. I know this is your first night off in a while." She's almost whispering, and from the way she's breathing, I'd say she's taken the call outside.

"It's okay, Ma. I was just heading home anyway. What's up?"

She sighs. "I was adding the latest expenses to the accounts like you taught me, and then I looked at the farm account. There's a couple grand missing that I can't find receipts for."

"Don't worry, Ma. I'm sure they're somewhere. I'll come over and stay the night, okay?"

"Are you sure?" I hear the relief in her voice.

"I'm sure, Ma. I'll see you in a bit."

I should have seen this coming. It's been a while since he last relapsed.

Fuck, this is the last thing I need right now.

9

JUDSON

"Mom, what on earth is in this jar?" I shout out from the pantry.

"Which one?"

I want to say all the jars because the shelf I'm staring at wouldn't look out of place in a science lab.

Neither jar has a label, so god knows how long they've sat here. Some look like pickled vegetables, but I can't be sure. Some could be jelly.

Damn, it's been so long since I've had a peanut butter and jelly sandwich. I move on from the jars to a different shelf. If I'd known I was coming on a survival expedition, I would have brought supplies.

"Never mind. You said it was next to the jars, but I can't find it."

She comes in and immediately finds the box, totally nowhere near where she said it would be.

I shake my head but can't help looking at my mom and smiling.

She gives me the box and picks another three boxes.

"Mom, can I please organize your pantry and label your stuff? This is a mess."

"It's only a mess when you don't know where things are.

Besides, if you organize it, I can guarantee you'll throw out that jar of pickled onions that only your uncle eats with his dinner at Christmas. I'll never hear the end of it."

"Mom, there is literally nothing here that resembles a jar of pickled onions."

"Precisely."

I follow her back to the kitchen, shaking my head again. Maybe it is best to leave it, even though the thought of a pantry without proper labels and date stamps makes my skin itch with the need to do something about it.

"Okay, so what are we making?" I ask.

My hours at the bar still leave me with plenty of free time. Even after chasing Pierre for yet another non-update, I find myself needing something to do.

I know exactly what I want to do. I want to go to Skyler's place and see how he's doing.

When I saw him at the bar last weekend, he looked tired, but I don't know if it's okay to just drop by unannounced again.

I shouldn't want to help him. It's one thing getting to know adult Skyler, but another one altogether to have the same feelings I had when I was a teenager and wanted to help him at the farm so he'd have more time to hang out.

That's not why I want to help him. I don't want to spend more time with him.

"I could ask for a dollar for your thoughts, but I don't need to." My mom slides a cup of coffee in front of me and sits on the opposite side of the kitchen table with her own cup.

"What? What do you mean?"

She raises a brow.

"Honey, it's just you and me here. Let's talk."

I groan. "I thought you needed my help."

She stares at me. Her eyebrow action today is fierce.

"This is a trap, isn't it?" I take a sip of the coffee. It's still too hot to drink, so I set it down while I try to figure out how to get out of this.

"I'm just going to say what I want to say because the last time I didn't, I ended up not seeing you for ten years."

"Mom..."

"I know you had a crush on Skyler when you were a teenager. Maybe even deeper than a crush. Is that why you left?"

I run my fingers through my hair, resting my elbows on the table.

"Yes, but not just that... Can we please not talk about it? It was a long time ago."

"Okay, so tell me, how do you feel now?"

"Confused. I should be angry. I *was* angry. But every time I see him, that anger is like a boiling pot of water evaporating until there's nothing."

She nods. "Do you think there may be something between you? That maybe he might feel the same way?"

I laugh. "What? No. He would never have feelings for me."

"Are you sure about that?"

I look up from my coffee cup. Those eyebrows sure are getting a workout today.

"Yeah, absolutely." Skyler is so in a different league. Even if I was interested, there's no way he'd take a second look at me. He probably still sees me as his short, fat friend.

"So what's your plan?"

I look outside the window behind my mom. Mud season has ended, and we're starting to get a hint of spring on the horizon. It's still fucking cold, but it's the kind of cold I'm used to.

Mom knows about Pierre and what happened in Paris. It seems that talking to Skyler at the cabin opened my box of secrets, and once I told him, I felt that I needed to tell my parents too.

My dad had gone apeshit, asking for all kinds of information and saying he'd sort it all out and I'd have my money in no time. Apparently, one of his work colleagues at the accountancy firm is married to a French woman whose brother is an accountant in Paris. It took everything in me not to break down in a sobbing mess because I couldn't remember the last time I had anyone so fiercely in my corner.

And that is totally my fault for practically running away ten years ago and staying away. The independence I needed to stand on my own two feet and find myself was good, but everyone needs someone to lean on every once in a while.

"My friend, Spencer, called me with a business proposal," I say.

Until I have my money from Pierre, I can't do anything, but maybe I can talk it through with my mom. After all, she's been my champion ever since I asked her to teach me how to cook.

"That sweet boy I met once on a video call?"

I laugh, remembering how my mom had become totally enamored with Spencer and his British accent. Not to mention he really is the most adorable person in the world.

"Yeah, him. He's been in LA for a while, and now that I'm Pierre-free—his words—he wants me to move there to work with him. He opened up a restaurant with his sister and wants to expand."

"So…you're leaving again?"

I hate to hear the disappointment in her voice, but what future do I have in Vermont? Whatever I choose to do, it's likely going to end up with me having to move.

"I don't know. Not yet, anyway. Spencer needs a business partner, and I don't have the capital. He's happy to wait for me though."

"Hmm…that's good…" She stands up and takes our empty cups with her to the sink. "If you're sure it's what you want, then I'll support you. I suppose at least you'll be on this side of the world. Maybe I can convince your dad to take a holiday and we can visit you on the West coast."

I go over to her and wrap my arms around her tiny frame. "I love you so much, Mom."

"Oh, I know. As moms go, I'm kinda neat."

I laughed. "You really are. Now tell me what it is we're supposed to be doing today."

She hands me the knife and points to the box of apples.

"We're decorating a cake and making mini apple pies for a retirement party. I already have the pastry in the fridge, so you can work on the filling while I work on the cake."

"Got it, Chef."

She laughs.

For the next hour or so, we work together with just the sound of her radio playing in the background. I plan in my head how I'm going to decorate the lattice cover for the pies.

I know it doesn't need to be anything complex, but it's been such a long time since I've worked with pastry that my body is practically humming with excitement.

My eye catches the bottle of Maple Sky syrup. Mom asked me to replace part of the sugar with maple syrup which turns out to be a genius idea. The filling for the pies has the rich sweet scent of maple and cinnamon, and suddenly the voices of all of my teachers from culinary school fill my brain.

"What's up?" Mom asks when she sees I've stopped moving the rolling pin over the pastry.

"I was just thinking about culinary school. When we start, we go back to basics. I can't tell you how many hours I spent chopping vegetables until my knife skills were perfect. It just came to me that in that search for perfection, we focus on what we need to learn and forget what we already know."

"That makes sense, but I'm not sure I'm following." She's covering the cake in butter icing, so she's not looking at me.

"How much maple syrup have I consumed in my life?"

"You don't want me to answer that, do you?" She laughs.

I'd throw something at her if I didn't respect the cake she's working on.

"Anyway. I can't remember the last time I used maple syrup in anything."

"I suppose in Europe they're more likely to use honey," she says, and she's right, but there was nothing stopping me from doing something different after I opened the restaurant with Pierre.

But I hadn't. It dawned on me that I'd been so eager to please Pierre, his parents, the fans of French cuisine, that I'd forgotten who I was. No wonder the food critic had slated my food.

"I know what I need to do, Mom. As soon as I have the money from Pierre, I'm moving to LA to work with Spencer. And this time, it'll be on my terms. My food. My decision."

She stops her palette knife midway to the cake and places it back on the bowl.

"In that case, you shouldn't miss the Maple Festival up in Fairlington. It might inspire you."

I'm not sure what to make of the way she's looking at me, but she might be right. It could inspire me to create new recipes.

If I can get time off from the bar, I'll go.

And look at me not even thinking about Skyler being there as a reason to attend the fest.

Go me.

10

SKYLER

The sky is gray. That's no surprise. After all, this is Vermont. But the atmosphere at the Maple Festival is anything but.

There's always this buzz, almost like an electrical current, that transfers from person to person as they walk around the festival, trying all the maple-flavored treats.

If maple could be turned into energy, this last week in April would be enough to supply the whole state of Vermont. That's how amazing this event is.

Fairlington isn't far from Burlington, only about forty-five minutes, but I stayed at a hotel last night so I could set up my stand first thing this morning.

Powered by strong coffee and excitement, I was one of the first vendors to arrive, setting up in the location I was sent to by the event coordinators.

I stand back for a moment to check my display.

There's a banner above the stand to indicate that I'm a winner from last year's maple products contest, and my winner's rosette is pinned to my apron.

Winning here isn't about the prize but the validation it gives.

My A-grade amber maple syrup has won the first prize in its category for the last three years, and I hope to take home the prize again. I submitted my product to the judging panel earlier this week.

I've been trying to secure exclusive supply to a few stores and being able to say I won first prize is definitely opening a few doors. Slowly but surely.

Claire, from Heaven Scent, waves at me. "Looks like I've already won my prize because I've got a front-row seat to the best eye candy in this festival," she says.

I flex an arm, and she pretends to faint. I like Claire. We met at my first festival and became good friends.

We flirt back and forth, which amuses her husband, who says she even flirts with the chickens. Based on how often I see her squeeze his butt, I think he finds her distraction with me a good reprieve.

"What do you think?" I ask. "I have a new display unit. A tree fell on my land and a friend helped me cut it to size."

She stands next to me. "I like it. It looks sturdy and reliable."

I snort. "Are you really talking about the unit?"

"No. I'm waiting for you to tell me if you finally found a nice man to flirt with. I'll start charging, you know?"

I gasp. "You wouldn't. I'm only a poor sugarmaker. All lonely in my cabin, waiting all year for this moment when I get to end my dry spell. With your husband's consent, of course."

"That sounds wrong on so many levels."

I turn around and can't help my grin when I see Jud standing a few feet away.

"You came," I say.

He shrugs. "I've been made aware that no self-respecting, Vermont-born and raised chef would miss this festival."

Claire's not very discreet cough next to me brings my attention back to her.

"Claire, this is my friend, Judson." And then I look at Jud. "Judson, this is my friend, Claire, and over there, praying for a swift death when the time comes, is Claire's husband, James."

Jud waves at both of them, and Claire turns around to go back to her stall. Not before mouthing *wow* and winking at me.

"Hey, Claire," I say to her. "Do a swap?"

"Your mom's favorite?"

"Yup."

"You got it, honeybun."

She places a few of her soaps in a bag and tucks it under my stall, taking a couple of bottles of maple syrup and cream for herself.

I love that I can trade stuff like that and take home some gifts for my mom. Normally, I don't have a chance to see the rest of the festival, so I get whatever is closest to me.

Thanks to Claire's soaps, I'm going to score my favorite dinners for at least a month.

"So, what's good here?" Jud asks.

"Where do I start? I'd love to take you around, but I'm kinda stuck in place here."

"Seems like you're in good company," he says, looking at Claire, who's unashamedly staring at us.

She waves, and I'd flip her the bird if there weren't children around.

I give Jud a map of the festival and point out a few places he might like to try.

Unfortunately, a customer interrupts us, and soon a line forms behind her, so Jud says he'll be back later and leaves me to work.

The next few hours are a rush of sales, talking to people, and offering samples of maple cream and syrup. Most people buy both after trying a sample of the maple cream on a piece of home-made bread that my mom baked specially for the festival.

That thing is like crack. You can't have just one sample, and when people find out I only sell at the farmer's market in Burlington and a couple other stores, they buy more than one jar.

There was never any doubt that this event would bring in much-needed income. But now, more than ever, I need it.

I try not to think about the conversation with my dad the last time I was home. He promised he isn't gambling, but he also couldn't explain the missing money. Add in how defensive he was about it, and all I can do is brace myself for what's coming.

He wouldn't put the farm at risk again. He promised, and to give him credit, he's kept his end of the bargain.

Nope, I'm not going to think about it. This is my time, and I'm going to enjoy being at the festival as long as I can.

There's always a quiet period around lunchtime when everyone flocks to the food tent. I can smell it from here. The maple bacon pizza, the pancakes from Barnsby Sugarhouse, maple doughnuts…the thought alone is making my belly rumble.

James usually does the lunch run for us, so after serving my last customer, I grab my wallet to take some money out for him.

"I think you're good for lunch," he says, pointing behind me.

I turn around, and Jud is there, holding a pizza box.

"I figured it would be hard to grab a break. I've done some food shows. I know you can go all day without eating, and that's not good for you."

All I can do is smile at him because I'm shocked that he'd think of me and bring me lunch.

"So…you want pizza…or shall I take—"

"Gimme." I interrupt, walking over to him and taking the box from his hands.

He laughs, and the sound settles in my chest. I like that sound.

As soon as I opened the box, one thing becomes clear. Jud has some negotiating skills, or Louie, the guy that runs the pizza stand, thinks he has a chance with him. Half the pizza is covered with maple-glazed bacon and the other half with maple-glazed vegetables. Louie never customizes pizza at the festival because he has to get them in and out of the oven too quickly to serve the hungry crowds.

Does he have a chance with Jud?

I think it at the same time that I look at Jud. His face is scrunched up.

"You don't like it, do you? I'm sorry. I shouldn't have assumed," he says.

"No. No. This looks amazing. I'm just shocked because Louie isn't the kind of guy to alter his toppings for just anyone."

Jud shrugs. "I may have flirted. And given him the kind of challenge a chef never backs down from."

"You…flirted?"

"Much to most people's disbelief, I am not the tongue-tied teenager I was ten years ago." He takes a slice from the box and folds the triangle slightly before taking a big bite.

My brain is catching up with Jud's words, but my dick has no such problem. My dick couldn't give a shit about whatever he says because I'm too busy staring at the way his mouth wraps around the slice of pizza. I groan when he licks his lips, catching a bit of maple syrup from the corner of his mouth.

"Are you gonna eat or just stare at me? Because I will eat all of this, even if I have to double my runs this week."

I slap his hand away and go for a veggie slice. "So tell me what kind of challenge you gave Louie."

Jud snorted. "I said I love playing with my toppings and asked him if he's ever tried glazing anything other than bacon."

I laugh so loud that people nearby turn their heads to face us. That gains me a few sales once my stand catches their attention.

Jud stands beside me, chatting to my customers about maple syrup and trading recipes.

By the time we return to the pizza, it's already cold, but that never stopped anyone, so I eat two more slices before I'm full enough.

"Thank you for reminding me about the festival," Jud says. "I can appreciate it in a totally different way now. When we were kids, it was all about stuffing our faces until half our body composition was syrup."

"Those were the days." I nod, thinking about how innocent we were, still untouched by the responsibilities of adult life.

"I'm going to have another look at the traders before I head home," Jud says.

We stand in silence for a moment. There's so much we still haven't said to each other, so much I haven't told him.

My mouth speaks for me before my brain is able to filter it. "Stay. I have a hotel room."

11

JUDSON

"I'm sorry?"

Did Sky just...no, I must have misheard.

"Fuck...um, what I mean is that I always stay in a hotel during the festival and this year the room I got happens to have two beds, so if you wanted to stay and check out the festival tomorrow, you could...stay, I mean. The pancake breakfast is the best thing ever."

Sky looks as flustered as I feel.

I raise my hand. "You could have led with pancake breakfast."

He smiles. "I didn't know you could be so easily persuaded."

And now I'm the one feeling my skin heat under my coat. Not to mention other parts of my anatomy.

"Carbs are life." I joke, but after this weekend, I know I definitely need to up my runs. Maybe check if I can afford to join a gym.

Sky's still smiling at me, and I wish I could read his mind and know what he's thinking right now.

"Good. Go explore and meet me here at seven," he says.

I do a salute and leave him to serve his customers. But not before I steal a chunk of bread with maple cream.

"Dessert," I say, walking away.

His laughter stays with me for the rest of the afternoon.

The festival is much bigger than I remember. I guess, as a kid, my sole focus was getting as much maple-flavored stuff in me as possible, so I never noticed the rest.

I end up walking out of the perimeter of the festival. All of the stores in the area have signs indicating that they've entered a contest and we can use the specified QR code to vote for them.

After voting for the ones I found the most interesting, I head back to the main festival area to check out the Craft and Specialty Foods Show.

From the size of the tent, it looks like staying till tomorrow is a good idea.

The place is buzzing with people. There's no discernible path to follow, so I look at the names on each of the stalls and visit the ones that pique my interest.

I think about my call with Spencer and how I can level up my recipes. I have the classic education, but looking at all the stuff on offer at the festival, I suddenly feel very stiff and stuck in the traditional cooking methods.

I pick up leaflets, try samples, take photos, and speak to as many people as I can.

The more I see, the more ideas start bubbling in my head. I almost wish I'd brought a notepad to write everything down.

The rest of the afternoon goes by in a heartbeat, and I have to pick up my pace to get back to Maple Sky by seven.

Sky has everything packed by the time I get to him, and he's ready to go.

"Sorry, am I late? I got distracted talking to someone about the best technique to glaze a large piece of ham."

He smiles, and I can't tell if he finds me amusing or a little weird. Probably a bit of both.

"Come on, Chef. Let's find dinner. I'm hungry," he says.

"Lead the way."

"What are you in the mood for?"

I think about it for a moment. I've already eaten way too much today. "I'm happy with anything as long as there's something light on the menu, like a salad or something."

He narrows his eyebrows.

"What?"

"Nothing… Come on. I know a place that makes really good locally sourced food."

Not surprisingly, there isn't a single item on the menu that doesn't have maple syrup in some form, but the BLT salad with the dressing on the side is definitely a better option for me.

My body was crying out for the fresh lettuce, and the maple-glazed bacon pieces taste divine.

"Are you sure that's enough for you?" Sky asks.

"Yeah, this is pretty good. I needed it after eating all those samples of everything maple."

Sky takes a bite of his massive burger with—you guessed it—maple-glazed bacon, double cheese, and maple barbecue sauce.

"Is it very difficult?" he asks as I'm finishing my salad.

"What?"

"Keeping the weight off."

"Not anymore. It's something I'm aware of because I don't want to go back to being the size I was, but I manage it."

He seems to think about something for a moment, and I'm not sure I want to talk about this. Losing the weight was one of the hardest things I did in my life. Being surrounded by food and being required to taste everything I cooked was my personal living hell.

But I did it, and I'm proud of what I look like now, even if I still have some hang-ups. I can't buy clothes online because I default to larger sizes. I need to try everything on because it's the only way my brain will accept that I fit into a smaller size.

"I never thought you were that big," Sky says, interrupting my thoughts.

"Were you blind?" I joke, but it's a deflection. How could he not see it? It's there in all the photos we took from when we were toddlers until high school.

A lump forms in my throat, and I really don't want to talk about my weight or my size issues. It always feels too raw.

"I wasn't blind, Jud. I saw you...you, not your size. So what if you were bigger than the other kids at school or me? You never let that stop you from doing anything."

Yes, it did.

I want to say it aloud so much, but instead, I ask the passing waiter for the bill.

We walk to the hotel in silence. It's cold, which gives me an excuse to wrap my scarf around my face.

"Jud. Talk to me. I said something wrong, didn't I?" Sky asks.

I stop on the sidewalk. Earlier today, the roads around the festival were filled with people, but now it almost feels a little eerie.

"You said my size never stopped me from doing anything, but that's not true. I went through high school without ever being kissed by another boy. I wasn't invited to parties unless you were. No one ever remembered my birthday. No one noticed my achievements. For someone so fucking big, I was so fucking invisible."

And this is the moment the well bursts. Fuck my life if I want to be crying in front of Sky West, my childhood best friend and current first contender for Superman lookalike. But that's what's happening.

I'm standing on a fucking sidewalk, in fucking Vermont, with tears running down my face as I stare at Sky's pity-filled hazel eyes.

I start walking again, even though I don't know where the hotel is. And now I'm regretting staying the night because I feel embarrassed enough without adding sleeping in close quarters with Sky.

"Jud." Sky pulls my arm with enough force that I end up turning around and crashing against him.

His eyes are dark and searching, his brows drawn together. He places his hands on either side of my face. "You were never invisible to me. Ever. Fuck, you were *all* I could see. The world could have vanished, and I'd have only noticed if you disappeared with it."

Being this close to Sky is dangerous. My heart is beating out of control, and my brain can't process the words Sky is saying with the memories it holds because they couldn't be farther apart than the two poles.

"Please let me go, Sky." Well, at least my mouth seems to be working.

He smiles, and I can tell it's because I've just used his nickname for the first time since we met again.

I'm in such deep shit.

"What if I don't want to?" he says.

What??

"What?"

"What if I want to put a smile back on your face?"

I think I'm having an aneurysm. That, or I've stepped into an alternative universe.

His smile turns into an evil grin. "Because I still remember how you loved when I did this—"

My scream pierces the quiet street as I bend over, giggling as Sky holds me in place and tickles me until tears run down my face for a new reason.

I'm sure I'd have a hard-on the size of Vermont if I wasn't so busy trying to breathe.

"You fucker," I say, trying to get away from his hold. "I'm going to get you for this."

He laughs. "I'd love to know how."

"Remember who you're sleeping next to." I wiggle my brows, and he gasps.

Sky sleeps like the dead, which, while we were growing up, gave me plenty of opportunities to spend hours staring at him during the night and to prank him.

Not that I'd do anything to him now, but he doesn't need to know that.

"Maybe this was a bad idea. How far away is your car? Burlington is only forty-five minutes away, and you'd sleep in your own bed…"

"Too late," I say. "You've already promised me pancakes for breakfast."

12

SKYLER

This is *it*. *This* is what I've been missing for ten years.

Laughing with Jud. Teasing him. Having fun.

It makes me angry that I missed out on ten years of friendship. It makes me angrier that I always wondered what would have happened after the graduation party if he hadn't left.

But the Jud I knew then is different to the one walking side-by-side with me listing all the things he'll do to me in my sleep.

"Dammit, a whole afternoon wasted being an adult when I could have bought supplies," he mutters under his breath.

"What?"

"Huh?"

"You said something about supplies," I say, trying to keep the edge off my voice so I don't give away exactly what kind of supplies I'm thinking about.

"Sharpies, superglue, glitter. How am I supposed to torment you in your sleep without supplies?"

"I say you torment me enough as it is."

He laughs.

"By the way, do you still snore? Because that's a hard limit for me. I need my beaut—humph" I cough to regain my breath after Jud punches me in the side.

"Jeez, you're stronger than you look."

"And you'd do well to remember it," he says. "And fuck you, I don't snore. As if you'd even notice if I did."

I put my arm around him in a headlock and mess up his hair.

"Dude!" he cries.

"If I wake up looking like a unicorn pooped on me, there will be repercussions."

"Ooh, so scared. Whatcha gonna do, big boy?" he teases back, and fuck if I'm not getting harder and harder in my jeans.

I let go of him and immediately feel the loss of his smaller body against mine.

The conversation we had earlier has been put aside, but I haven't forgotten. I just can't allow myself to think about how broken and hurt Jud sounded. Because I'll want to do something about it, and right now, there's only one way I could show him how very not invisible he is to me.

And that's a door that needs to remain shut.

My hotel room isn't huge, but it does have two beds and its own bathroom. I thought there was plenty of space, but now with Jud here, it suddenly feels too small.

I feel like my secrets are going to spill out just by the fact we're going to breathe the same air for the next eight hours.

He walks over to the window to look at the street below. I picked this hotel because they let me park my truck at the back after I unload for the festival and it's central enough that I can walk everywhere I need to for the weekend.

"This is nice. Thanks for letting me stay with you," he says.

"You're welcome. I...I think there's a spare toothbrush in the bathroom. I could use a shower, but I can wait if you want to go first."

Jud stares at me wide-eyed. "No, no, it's your room. You go first."

I nod and go into the bathroom, closing the door behind me.

I don't wait until the water is warm before I step inside the shower. My body is probably wondering why I hate it so much, but this is what I need.

If everything is cold, there's less chance of me embarrassing myself in front of Jud.

Just as the water starts warming up, I'm done. It's not like I've been working at the farm, so I'm not that dirty.

I step out and grab a towel to dry myself, and that's when I realize that in my haste to get away from Jud, I forgot to bring any clothes or underwear.

"Take a deep breath, Sky. You can do this. Just wrap the towel around your waist, think of the time it'll take to clean up the tubing system next week." As soon as I feel safe that the thought of doing that work is enough to keep me from springing wood, I do as I say.

I wrap my towel around my waist as tight as possible and go back out into the room.

Jud is still by the window in the same place I left him. He turns around and gasps, looking immediately away.

"Sorry," he says.

"No, I'm the one who's sorry. I forgot to take clothes with me."

He points at the door. "Is it… Can I?"

"Yeah, go ahead."

As soon as Jud is safely on the other side of the door, I put some underwear on, adding a pair of sweatpants for good measure. I don't bother with a T-shirt because the sweatpants alone will make me overheat. I normally sleep just in my boxer shorts or naked if I'm horny, but tonight there's no way I'm risking any less than two layers of clothing down there.

I turn the lights off since there's enough glare from the street lights outside and get under the covers. I hear the toilet flushing, and a moment later, Jud comes out, and I get the answer to the question I've wanted to ask since I saw his tattooed arm at the bar.

Everywhere. His tattoos are fucking everywhere, and I've never in my life wanted to touch someone as much as I want to touch him right now.

In the relative darkness of the room, he can't see me staring at him, which is just as good because I don't think I could handle looking into his eyes too.

Jud tries to use a towel to cover himself up, and I hate that he feels self-conscious about his body when mine is reacting to it so fiercely that I think I would probably be arrested for my current thoughts alone.

I still manage to see the ink he has all over his chest, down his trim belly, and hiding under his boxer shorts. There's some on his legs, too, but not as much.

I turn around to face the wall.

The confusion and sadness I've carried with me in the last ten years are evaporating faster than I expected, and I don't understand it.

He left out of the blue without saying goodbye. We were friends. Jud and Sky, inseparable from the moment we were born. And then it was just me, without my friend to lean on when I needed him the most.

I should still be angry. Why am I not?

"Night, Sky," he says, and I hear the sounds of the bedsheets as he gets into bed.

"Night, Jud."

I'm still confused as hell the next morning when Jud is quiet even through our pancake breakfast.

He makes all the right sounds and even chats with an old lady sitting next to us about the ratio of pancake to syrup to fruit. He argues that those fluffy pancakes need Nutella on them more than life needs water.

I snort as the lady looks at him like he's the devil incarnate, and I can't say I disagree with her.

I'm from Vermont, so it would be sinful to have anything but maple on my pancakes, but I have tried chocolate spread, and as nice as it was, it's not the same.

I'll die on that hill, even though I would be happy to compromise and allow a jar of Nutella to live side-by-side with my maple syrup just to make Jud happy.

Um…what now?

Jud's phone rings, taking me out of my stupid thoughts.

"Hey, Oz," he says, answering the phone.

Oz is one of the bartenders at Vino. Jud smiles, and I can't help feeling a little jealous that I haven't seen that smile directed at me today.

"Yeah, sure. I can cover for you. Okay, bye now."

He puts the phone back in his pocket. "I have to go back this morning. Oz needs me to cover his shift today, and I need the money, so…"

"That sucks, but that's adulting for you. Gotta do the right thing, yes?"

"Yeah." He looks down at his plate and pushes it away.

I don't feel hungry anymore either.

I don't even know why I'm disappointed that Jud is leaving early.

It's not like he could stay another night. He doesn't even have clean underwear or more clothes.

It's not like we'd be able to spend any time together. Saturday is the busiest day of the festival, so I won't be free until tonight and, by then, he'd be gone anyway.

Claire greets me with an all-knowing smile and a large coffee in a takeout cup. "This is yours if I get the dirty on your sexy friend with the blue eyes."

"You forget that I also had the pancake breakfast."

"You forget that I know how substandard the coffee there is compared to how heavenly the pancakes are."

Claire was there with James, too, but their family is here for the festival, which means she couldn't join us to grill Jud over breakfast.

"Damn you, woman." I take the coffee from her and take a sip. "Ahh, this is going to keep me going for the rest of the day."

Claire crosses her arms and taps her feet, waiting.

"There's nothing to tell. We're just friends."

She laughed. "The last time a *friend* looked at me like that, I ended up marrying him."

"Damn right, baby," James says, giving her a high five.

I sigh. "Okay, later, because it looks like I've got customers."

The rest of the weekend flies past. I sell out and spend the final hours of the festival handing out business cards with my website details and also where people can find me to buy Maple Sky.

By the time I pull up at my parents, I'm exhausted but dying to show them my new winner's rosette. I'm on top of the world and feel like nothing can stop me from taking my business to the next level.

That is until I go inside.

13

JUDSON

There's been a weird atmosphere in the bar since the panels covering the front of the hostel came down.

Because it's across the street from Vino, it's within eyesight, and naturally, people want to talk about it. What's weird is that people are whispering to each other every time they look over at the newly painted façade.

I don't want to pry, but I'm curious.

My memories of the old hostel are very vague. I just remember it being there and never paying particular attention. I mean, why would I?

"Hey, Oz, mind if I ask you a question?"

Oz finishes pouring a glass of 2011 Château de Mont Pérat for a customer and then joins me.

"What's up?"

"What's the deal with the hostel? Why is everyone whispering as if they're not allowed to talk about it? Have they found out it's haunted or something?"

Oz looks around the bar and then at the door to the kitchen before he turns back to me.

"Nah, it's not haunted...at least, I don't think it is. You know

Jax was living there when the place burned down, so I guess it's still a little raw, and people respect both him and Tanner."

I nod. "Yeah, I get it. Do you think it's opening again? It doesn't really look like a hostel. Did it always have that big window at the front?"

"No, I guess they made it bigger. Who knows what's happening," he shrugs.

We each go back to our own thing. Oz is a cool guy. Very chill and easy to talk to.

The cook rings the bell, and because I'm free, I go into the kitchen to check which food order is ready.

Much in the same way I've settled into the job, my relationship with the cook has improved greatly. I apologized for breaking the chef code, and he seems to have forgiven me.

After I brought him a bottle of maple barbecue sauce from the festival, he declared me his best friend. Yup, chefs are that easily bought.

I load the plates on a tray and take them out to the table.

Anita, Noah, and their friends come in as I'm clearing one of the booths.

"Mademoiselle," I say with a flourish, pointing at the clean table.

"Ooh, I could get used to this," she says.

"Thanks, man," Noah says.

I'm introduced to Wyatt and Andy, who I've seen here before but haven't been formally introduced to.

"Looks like Skyler's going to be late," Wyatt says, looking at his phone.

"I didn't realize he was coming tonight," I say.

Anita smiles and gives me a scrutinizing look, not dissimilar to the ones I get from my mom. Is it a mom thing? Do you get it after you've given birth? Or is it a woman thing?

"Right...um, I better get back to the bar. If you're looking for something to eat, specials are on the board. I'm not gonna say I've tried the potato, bacon, and mozzarella fingers and loved them, but I'm not, *not* gonna say it if you know what I mean."

They laugh.

"Hey, if you have a break coming up, why don't you join us?" Andy asks.

"Thanks, I do, actually. I can take your orders and bring them on my way back."

At my advice, they order double portions of the fingers, much to the cook's delight. This is a new thing he's trying to see if customers go for it. He makes his own chili dip, which has just the right heat level for me.

My break comes up just as their food is ready, so I take my salad from the staff fridge and plate it up. I don't want to be eating from a box in the bar.

The group is deep in conversation when I sit in the booth next to Anita.

"Hey, Judson, have you seen anything? You're here more often," Noah asks.

"Seen what?"

"You know. The TV people," Andy says.

"I have no clue what you're talking about. What TV people?"

Wyatt leans forward as if he's going to share a secret.

"After the hostel burned down, the owners took the insurance money and moved away. I've heard rumors that the mayor wants to repurpose it because it's in a prime location."

"That makes sense," I say.

"Yes, but it's costly work. Nothing happened for months, but then the mayor was in talks with a local TV channel to produce a reality TV show based here."

I stared at Wyatt. A reality TV show? I can't think of anything worse than having cameras around Burlington all the time.

He continues. "So...it's not public yet. I know this because a girl I work with is dating a guy that works in the mayor's office, and she told me..."

He pauses for effect, and I want to snort at the theatrics, but I don't know the guys that well and don't want them to get offended or think I'm rude.

"They've been planning this for months…"

"Oh, just spill it," Anita says, taking the last potato finger and dipping it in the sauce.

"You're no fun," Wyatt moans.

"Oh, she's plenty of fun," Noah says, and both Wyatt and Andy groan.

"Thanks, babe. And that's why I married you," she says.

"I thought it was because of—" Anita slams her hand over Noah's mouth and gives him a warning look.

I can't help laughing. These guys are funny. I can see why Sky is friends with them.

"My break is ending soon, don't leave me hanging, Wyatt," I beg.

"Fine, fine. There's going to be a reality TV show that is supposed to put Church Street on the Vermont foodie roadmap. The mayor wants this to be a major stop for people seeking new food experiences. It looks like the first floor will be converted into a restaurant for the show, and the upper floors will be repurposed as kitchen labs that can host cooking classes afterward. Sounds like they want teams with a minimum of two people competing."

"Why?" Anita asks.

"Don't know. Because it makes for more interesting TV if people argue and things get heated during the show? Who knows," Wyatt says.

I sit back and look at the building across the road.

"I think that's a great idea. Apart from the whole TV show, that is."

"Oh my gosh, you and Skyler should totally enter the show," Anita says, almost shrieking with delight. "With your cooking knowledge and his maple products, you'd totally win."

"Whoa, no way, I'm *not* going to be on TV."

"But if you win, imagine what it could do to your career and Skyler's business. You'd sky rocket into success," she says.

I smile at her and kiss her cheek. "Thank you for believing we'd be good enough to enter, but I've got to get back to work."

She pouts, and I pout back at her before taking the empty plates and bottles. "I'll buy your next round."

The bar gets so busy that I end up forgetting about the group until Sky turns up just before we close. I look around, and his friends have left, but he's not looking for them.

He comes straight to the bar and sits on a free stool.

"Hey, what can I get you?" I ask.

"Can I have a soda?"

"Sure. Are you okay?"

He looks exhausted. I thought he'd have a break now that tapping season has ended.

After the festival, I didn't see him for a week until he came into the bar with his friends for a quick drink one night. I thought it would be awkward seeing him after spending the night in the same room, but there was no weirdness between us.

I was gutted when I realized I missed seeing him win his prize, but Oz needed cover, and I need all the money I can get my hands on.

With Pierre being a total dick, I'm starting to believe I'll need to hire a lawyer.

"What time do you finish?" Sky asks.

"In fifteen minutes. I'm not on cleaning duty tonight. Why?"

"Want to grab a late burger?"

"Sure."

I leave Sky with his drink and go clear some tables to help out the guys on closing duty.

There's a place not far from Vino that stays open late, so when I finish my shift, I grab my stuff and meet Sky outside.

"You look beat. Why aren't you home in bed?" I ask.

He sighs and then shrugs. "I don't want to be on my own in the cabin, and I don't want to go home."

I put my arm around his. "Come on, let's go eat an early-grave burger. It'll make you feel better."

"I know. That's why I invited you."

14

SKYLER

Jud tells me to sit at a table while he gets the burgers, and I'm so glad to not have to make another fucking decision today that I do what I'm told.

Unless he gets me a fish burger. I might need to reconsider our friendship in that case.

I'm lost in my fish burger thoughts when a proper real-life double cheeseburger, with bacon and a side of fries, appears in front of me, followed by an actual milkshake.

"Is it chocolate peanut butter?" I ask, but I don't let Jud answer. I get that straw in my mouth and suck on it, waiting to be proven right when the delicious flavor hits my tastebuds. "Hmm, fuck, this is good. Thank you. What do you have?"

"Same milkshake and a portion of chicken fingers. I had dinner earlier, so I'm not that hungry."

I bite my burger, and the salty, meaty, juicy flavors are so tasty, I can't help moaning and taking a second bite straight away.

"When was the last time you ate?" Jud asked, laughing.

"Lunch," I say with my mouth full of food.

"Gross."

I smile, and he picks up one of my fries and pretends to throw it at me but eats it instead.

"You look tired, Sky. Are you still at your cabin?"

I shake my head and swallow my food. "I'm traveling back home every day."

"Why? Has your season ended already?"

"Just. The taps are dry now, so it's clean-up time."

Jud stares at me, and I know what he's thinking. When I gave him the tour of the sugar house, I talked about the post-season work, which involves removing all the tubing, cleaning it and storing it for another year, and making sure all the taps are removed so the trees can heal.

"What's going on?"

I take a deep breath and put my burger down on the plate.

"My dad relapsed. He'd been gambling. Mostly small money, but a few weeks ago, we found two grand missing, and then when I got back from the festival, there were additional funds in the account."

"He won the money back."

I nod. "He promised he wouldn't gamble again, but I can't believe him now. I'm afraid to turn around and see us lose everything. This time for good."

Jud puts his hand on mine and squeezes.

"Maybe he'll keep his promise. Can you take away his access to the business accounts?"

"I can, but…" I'm not sure how to explain it. This is my dad I'm talking about. He was the person I looked up to growing up, and it doesn't feel right to treat him like an errant child, even if it's for his own good.

"Sky, you're not emasculating your dad; you're protecting him. He must understand that."

How is it possible Jud gets me so well? I don't even have to say it for him to know how I feel.

"I just…I feel so stuck. I'm twenty-eight years old, and I run a successful business that has potential for expansion. But I still live at home and can't afford to take risks with my life in case it's sabotaged again."

"When is Miles coming home?"

"End of summer. He's doing his finals now, and then he has a couple of months left at the farm, although he says he may be back earlier. I don't know."

Jud eats his last piece of chicken and puts the plate aside, sipping on his milkshake.

"Tell me about your expansion plans."

I snort. "They're more like pipe dreams than plans."

"Doesn't matter. They're *your* dreams. No one can take that away from you, and no one should do anything but cheer you along the way."

A little bubble of excitement is already building inside me. I love talking about my plans, even if sometimes I don't believe they'll actually come through.

"My goal is to open a store. Have an actual physical space rooted to the ground. A place where I can sell Maple Sky and other locally sourced products. I've seen a few empty units on Church Street get snapped up over the years because I didn't have the down payment required for the rent. Not to mention that I can't be in a store full-time while I still work for my dad, and I definitely can't afford to hire anyone to work for me. I'd probably start off with short opening hours after maple season and work through the year to build..." I look at Jud, and he's staring at me with a strange expression. "What?"

"You can do it, Sky. I know you can," he says.

"Yeah, in about five years." I sigh.

"Maybe not."

"What do you mean? Are you hiding a winning lottery ticket in your jacket or something?"

He rubs his face and exhales. "I can't believe I'm saying this... Do you want to enter a reality TV show with me?"

It takes me a while to stop laughing and see the very unimpressed look from the people sitting at nearby tables.

I look at my phone. "It's late. Are you overtired? Maybe delirious? What did they put in your chicken fingers?"

"I'm not joking." To give him credit, he's not even smiling. In fact, he looks absolutely terrified, as if he'd take the words back if he could.

"You're not joking."

He shakes his head.

"Okay, from the beginning."

Jud tells me what he heard from Wyatt earlier, and I'm not sure if I want to kill my friend or thank him for the information.

And that's how, two weeks later, Jud and I find ourselves in the large room where they hold meetings at the town hall.

The website Wyatt sent us was so basic that we couldn't really tell what the show was about. All we know is that we have to enter in teams of at least two and each team will be filmed running a pop-up restaurant for a week.

We, alongside all the candidates who passed the online assessment, are sitting in the center of the hall, and all around us are desks where we'll be called over for an interview.

Our names are called, so I stand up, but Jud is rooted in place.

"Hey, you okay?"

"Yeah, just…nervous. I mean, we're going to be on camera and—"

"Hey." I kneel beside him. "Let's just talk to this person and see what the show is about. Let's face it, we're unlikely to be picked, right? It'll be a fun story to tell your grandchildren."

Jud smiles and stands up, holding my hand and not letting go until we take our seats in front of a woman who has a plaque on her desk that reads *Producer*.

"Welcome." She grabs some papers. "So you're Skyler and Judson, right? I'm Samantha, and I'm one of the producers of the show. How are you?"

"A little nervous," Jud says.

Her smile is warm and reassuring. "That's perfectly natural. There's a reason I'm behind the camera, not in front of it, that's Yolanda's job. But I can assure you we have a team of professionals who will always make sure you're looking your best. Now, tell me a little bit about you."

We look at each other, and I see the plea in Jud's eyes.

I turn to Samantha. "Jud is a chef. He trained in London and then moved to Paris, where he worked in a few prestigious restaurants."

"Oh, how interesting. And what brings you to Vermont?" She asks, turning to Jud.

"Um, I'm from here. Sky and I grew up together. Um...things in Paris didn't work out, and I guess I missed home, so...here I am."

I squeeze his arm. I'm not sure why he's nervous because I'm pretty sure we're not getting picked.

"Hmm, home is important. Coming back to your roots and all. How about you, Skyler? What do you do?"

"I'm a farmer and a sugarmaker. I help run my family's dairy farm, but I also run my own business. I sell my own maple syrup and other derivatives."

She writes a few notes before saying, "So, a chef and a sugarmaker. You could make an interesting team. Our viewers would love you. And you both already look great."

I laughed. "What?"

She raises her head. "Skyler, TV is all about visual entertainment. You two make a great couple visually. Let's hope we see your chemistry come through on screen."

"Our what?" Jud sits up straighter, and Samantha smiles.

"We have cameras everywhere here. We've been observing you since the moment you came in. Don't worry, we couldn't hear your conversation. We just want to see how natural you are with each other. You won't be surprised to hear many similar shows hire actors to fill some of the contestant spots. We're not like that. I've been on the production team of a couple of reality shows: one about sewing and crafts and one about woodworking. I guarantee not everything you see on TV is one hundred percent genuine. Now...there's something I need to know."

ANA ASHLEY

We both nod.

"Are you engaged? Already married?"

15

JUDSON

"I'm sorry, what?"

"We're not together."

Sky and I say at the same time.

Samantha sits back in her chair and laughs. "Well, whatever you are, it'll play great on camera."

"What do you mean?" I ask.

She ignores my question. "Okay, so this is how it's going to work. Here's a folder with all the information you need to know about the restaurant. The layout of the dining area, kitchen, how to get stock delivered, opening hours. Basically, anything you need to know about the daily running has already been decided to make it consistent across all contestants."

"Wait," Sky says. "Does that mean we're in?"

"Honey, you've been in since the moment you walked in looking like that," she says, waving her hand in a circular motion in front of us.

I'm not sure what she means. I mean, Sky will look great on camera because he's drop-dead gorgeous, but surely this is about the restaurant and the eating experience.

She keeps talking about the rules and line-ups and schedules, and it dawns on me that we're missing a key piece of information.

"Samantha, I'm sorry to interrupt, but what's the winning prize?"

"Oh, silly me. We kept it vague in the signup sheet on purpose to avoid attracting time-wasters. The winning team will get a year-long free lease of the restaurant and the upper floors with first refusal when the lease is up for renewal."

I look at Sky, and he's frozen, still staring at Samantha. This is what he wants. This is his dream.

"So, boys. Are you in, or are you—"

"We're in," we say in unison.

She laughs. "Perfect. Filming will start next week. We want to see as much of your day-to-day interactions and planning as possible before your week is up at the restaurant."

My hands shake as I sign the contract, and looking at Sky, he's not doing much better.

We walk out of the town hall in silence, neither of us saying anything until we're in front of Vino.

I have an idea, so I grab Sky's hand and pull him to the bookstore.

We walk past the checkout desk and wave at Briar, who's ringing up a purchase. Sometimes I come over before starting my shift at the bar to look at their selection of cookbooks, and I've seen him with a group of people, talking about the books they've read.

I've always enjoyed reading, especially crime fiction. But with the schedule I kept as a chef, my body clock rarely aligned with most people's, so I never bothered joining a book club.

"What are we doing here?" Sky asks.

"First things first. Coffee? I can't get you anything stronger at this time of day."

"Coffee would be good, thanks."

I grab us drinks from the coffee counter and bring them back to the comfy couches in the event area. We take up a three-seater and face each other. I'm glad there aren't any events going on right now, so apart from a few people browsing, it's fairly quiet around us.

"Are we really doing this?" Skyler whispers, looking around as if to ensure we're not overheard.

"I guess we are. Are you as freaked out as I am?"

He nods.

I'm holding the folder with all of the information, so I open it between us.

The more I read, the more confident I become about our chances at winning this. Ideas take form in my head quickly, and I realize I need to write them down.

"Where are you going?" Sky asks.

"Just buying a notebook. I'll be right back."

I walk over to the desk where there's a range of fancy notebooks, but I'm looking for something a little less expensive.

"Can I help you with anything?" Briar asks.

"Yeah, I need a notebook, but nothing fancy. I just want to write down some stuff, and it'll probably end up with coffee stains on it, so I don't want to spend much money on it."

He points at a small display on the opposite side of the checkout desk, and I see a range of chicken-themed stationery. I remember Molly telling me how Harrison, the owner of V&V, met his now-boyfriend after some confusion over a chicken delivery.

The pictures on all the items are ridiculously adorable, and I have to contain myself to not spend money I really don't have.

I grab a notepad and a pen and pay for it. On my way back to Sky, I notice he looks a little lost in himself.

"Hey, you okay?"

He nods and smiles at me. I try not to think about how amazing it feels every time Sky smiles at me.

"Okay so, clearly there are a few things we need to do on this list, but let's put that to one side. I think we have a real shot at this," I say.

"You do?"

"Yeah."

"How? How are you so confident?"

"Because, my dear friend, I didn't become the youngest hot thing in the Paris restaurant scene for nothing. Well, before my reputation got shredded to pieces, of course. Anyway, we're going to win this because I know food, you own the main attraction, and we both know how to run a business."

I don't think Sky's smile could get any wider. His hair has grown a little longer since I met him that first night at the bar. His beard is longer than a little scruff, and I wonder how it would feel to…

Sky coughs, and I jump back on the couch.

How did we get so close?

"Um…yeah, so I have some ideas for recipes we can try." I open my notebook and unscrew the cap on the pen I just bought.

Sky puts his hand on my chin to make me face him.

"I really wanted…I mean, I could have just…Jud…" His voice is almost a whisper, and my brain is desperate to fill in the missing words. *To kiss you…kissed you…*

"Sky…"

"I know…I know…"

Why do I feel like we're having a conversation without saying anything at all? And how do I find out if what he's not saying is exactly what I'm thinking and not just what I want him to say?

Fuck my life and the stupid crush I have on Skyler West. This would be so much easier if he were straight. Why isn't he fucking straight like he was back in high school?

Because he was never straight.

"What?" he asks, and that's when I realize I must have mumbled my thoughts aloud.

"I need to go. My shift at the bar is starting soon. We should meet again soon to go over the details."

He stands up. "Okay. When's your next day off?"

"Tomorrow."

"Meet me at my parents' at ten."

"Okay."

I'm left staring at the blank page of my new notebook.

I really should spend less time around Sky, *not* more, and definitely not in front of TV cameras.

"Okay, Jud. New plan. Practice looking unaffected by the sexy man with the big muscles and the killer smile."

"Good luck."

I look up, and Briar is working on a nearby display, putting some books back.

"I'm sorry, what?" I ask.

"Good luck with your self-imposed plan." He's smiling like he's in on something I'm not.

"What do you mean?"

"You can try to look unaffected by someone, but unless you *feel* unaffected, your plan won't work."

I suck in a breath and let it out slowly. "It has to work. He can't know."

"Why?"

"Because…because…I don't even know anymore. He hurt me a long time ago, but…"

"Do you still feel hurt?" Briar asks.

I shrug. "I don't know. When I think of that day, I do. I feel it so much, but then I look into his eyes, and I don't know."

"Maybe it's not important anymore. You can spend a lifetime arguing which one is better, doughnuts or crullers. In the end, all that matters is that they're both sweet."

I don't understand his reference, but it makes sense.

"I'm sorry. I don't know why I'm offloading on you like this."

"Sometimes it's easier to talk to strangers."

Briar leaves me to go back to his books, and I grab my things to head over to the bar.

I think of Briar's words throughout my shift, but my insecurities still hover over me like a sad cloud.

By the time I get home, I'm even more annoyed with myself. My mom tries to stop me to chat, but I use my tiredness as an excuse. I'll need to speak to her in the morning about the show, but first, I need to give myself a good talking to.

16

SKYLER

I run down the stairs as soon as I see Jud's car approaching the farmhouse.

"Whoa, where's the fire?"

I slide to a stop in my socks and laugh. "Hey, Ma. You look gorgeous today."

She raises a brow.

"What? I haven't asked you for any food."

"Yet."

I sidle up to her and wrap my arm around her shoulders. She's so tiny against me. It's crazy when I think about how both Miles and I are so tall compared to her. Then again, my dad isn't exactly short.

She pats my chest.

"Do you want me to prepare you boys a packed lunch?"

I bat my eyelashes and give her a kiss on the cheek. "If you're offering. I'm sure our guest would appreciate your kind gesture."

She shakes her head and goes to the kitchen.

I put my boots on and open the door to meet Jud, who's already at the top of the stairs.

"Hi," he says.

"Hi.

"I brought my notebook so we can plan...um...stuff."

I raise a finger. "First, you need to see what we have." I look at what he's wearing, and it's suitable enough, apart from his shoes.

"See what you have?"

I take the notebook from his hands and give him my spare boots.

"Okay, I'm scared now," he says, putting the boots on and tying the laces tight. I think they're a little too big for him, but they'll do.

"Don't be. It's still mud season here, and you don't want to ruin your shoes. Come on."

He follows me out of the house and along the path that leads to my mom's garden.

"Wow, this hasn't changed at all," he says.

"Nothing much changes around here. Everything's functional."

"You say that like it's a bad thing. Isn't that how working farms are supposed to be?"

I shrug. "Yeah, I guess. It doesn't matter. This is going to be Miles's kingdom one day anyway."

"I prefer your forest," he says. "It's...cleaner."

I laugh. "I think you've hit the nail on the head. The forest is as organic as it can be. I clear it up for easy access and to prevent forest fires in the summer. I like sitting on the porch of the cabin and looking out to the undisturbed trees. Here, everything within walking range is used for something."

I open the gate to the garden and let Jud through before closing it again because Mom lets the chickens roam free.

"The asparagus, artichokes, and rhubarb are almost ready, and I think by the time we start filming, we'll have greens and potatoes. Mom also grows strawberries, and we have a few boysenberry plants, but those are harder to tell if we'll have a good crop or not."

"What do you mean?"

"I've spoken to Mom. Consider this your own storage room. From the source to the table with flair. I get the easy job. You have to add the flair."

Jud's smile competes with the spring sun lighting up the garden. He kneels on the soil, seemingly uncaring about his clothes, and takes a closer look at the vegetables.

"This is...wow...this is...I don't even have words."

Jud's happiness and enthusiasm make me feel things I shouldn't feel. He's just excited because we have a chance to offer locally sourced produce in the restaurant.

"But...what about your mom? Won't she need this?"

"This is mostly for us, but normally there's too much. We end up giving it away to friends, or my mom pickles some vegetables and makes chutneys. Do you think we'll have enough here to support our week at the restaurant?"

He stands up and comes over to me. There's a small dirt mark on his cheek from where he must have touched his face.

I bring my hand up to clean it, and he goes still. His eyes go a little dark, and we're back in the same place we were yesterday at the bookstore.

Fuck.

"Um...yeah, I haven't created the full menu yet, but...um...I think...it's enough."

The way he says it's enough makes me wonder if he's talking about something else.

I take my hand away and put it in my pocket before I do something stupid like hold his.

"Come on. There's something else I want to show you, but we need to stop at the house first."

"Okay."

As if she knows we're coming, my mom is on the porch steps with a bag in her hand, the motorcycle keys, and two helmets.

"Thanks, Ma."

"Will you boys be back in time for dinner?"

"We will, Ma."

"When have I heard that before?" she mutters before going back inside.

I go around the house and uncover our means of transportation.

"You have a bike," Jud says, going around the motorcycle and running his fingers over the leather seat.

"I do. She's an old lady, but she's never let me down."

We get the helmets on, and then I straddle the bike, giving enough space for Jud to get behind me.

I've never had anyone on the bike with me, and now I know why. The roar of the engine, the bumps in the uneven terrain, and Jud pressing his body against mine are a recipe for disaster, and I'm not even a chef.

Fortunately, by using the bike to get around, we arrive at our destination within a few minutes.

My parents' land has been passed down for generations on my mom's side, but the part we're in was bought by my grandparents, who were hoping to have a big brood and wanted plenty of space for all of their children to be able to build their own houses on the land.

The brood started and stopped with my mom, and after taking over the farm with my dad, my parents were so busy running it on their own that they didn't have much time to work out what to do with the land that wasn't used.

Jud gets off the bike, holding onto my arm for balance, and then I do the same, making sure the stand is in place so the bike doesn't topple over.

"What is this place?"

"We're at the edge of the property. Miles found this place years ago. He was doing a project for school, mapping the land and all the interesting features." I point to the far distance. "That's Mt. Mansfield."

Jud gazes at the view, and I know he sees exactly what I saw the first time I was here. This is Vermont. Trees as far as the eye can see, snowy peaks in the distance, and it's so peaceful you're almost afraid to say anything aloud that will disturb the magic of the place.

"This is where Miles is going to build his house," I say, pointing at the various wooden stakes Miles and I stuck in the ground to mark the boundaries of the house when he was last here.

We spent days coming here to catch the sunrise and the sunset to maximize sunlight in the house once it's built.

"How about you?"

I look at Jud. He's next to me in a light jacket because it may be spring, but this is still Vermont, and his hands are in his pockets. The way the sunlight hits his face makes his blue eyes brighter.

"When he's back, I'll move to the cabin permanently. That's my home. I don't know how to explain it, but I like it there among the trees. I feel more peace. In some ways, the two places aren't all that different, but here, all I feel is this weight pulling me down."

"At your place you have control over what happens. No one can let you down."

He does it again. Just like at the burger place, Jud sees through me better than I could if I was staring at myself in the mirror.

Does he see other things too?

"Come, I want to show you something else."

He follows me in silence, and I lead him through the trees. Once we get to the right spot, I let him pass me.

My eyes stay on his face as we turn the corner and he sees row after row of cherry trees.

His face lights up with the biggest smile possible as we walk to the middle of the orchard, where there's a strategically placed old tree log.

"I...I have no words. Sky, this is beautiful."

Weeks ago, the trees were full of bloom, but now the cherries are only a few weeks away from harvest, so there aren't as many blossoms.

"It's pretty impressive, isn't it?"

"I bet you bring all the boys he—" he trips on a small rock because he's still wearing my oversized boots.

I grab his hand just in time to stop him from falling, but I accidentally pull him with a little too much force, and he ends up facing me, chest to chest.

There's a battle going on inside me. My heart and my brain are at odds with each other, and I don't know which one to listen to.

Jud's eyes focus on mine before they travel down, and my resolve is broken as I close the distance between us and press my lips against his.

He's soft and warm. This feels so fucking right, and I haven't even tasted him. I pull away reluctantly and rest my forehead on his as I answer him.

"No, just one boy."

17

JUDSON

I knew I was gay when I was twelve and my heart suddenly started beating faster every time Sky was around. Even though I was confused about all the changes happening to my body, I knew one thing. I loved Skyler West.

That became my secret. And within the safety of my secret thoughts, I often allowed myself to dream.

What would it be like to be held by Sky? Not when we were messing around, but if he really wanted to just hold me close.

What would it be like to kiss him? Feel his lips on mine? Taste him?

My eyes are still closed, and I'm too scared to do or say something that will make him take it back.

He kissed you first. Sky kissed you first.

"Fuck it," I say and go in for another kiss. Whatever is happening right now, one thing's for sure. I want to go home with the taste of Skyler West imprinted on my brain.

It starts with small tentative kisses as if we're learning each other.

I always thought if I ever kissed Sky, it would be over so quickly that I'd need to take all I could with one kiss.

But no. Every time I try to deepen it, he slows down.

Sky's lips are so soft, and every time he opens his mouth slightly, I feel his warm breath.

This is so fucking frustrating. I want to do things to him with my tongue. How the fuck am I supposed to taste him?

He pulls back again, but he puts his finger over my lips. I take the message. He doesn't want me to talk and ruin the moment.

Fine. I smile against his finger and then suck it into my mouth without breaking eye contact.

The growl coming from his chest makes me feel so goddam powerful.

His eyes darken, and then his mouth is on mine again, but this time, he gives me everything I want.

I wrap my arms around his shoulders and grab his hair to keep him close. He's not fucking going anywhere until I've had enough, and that could be a long time.

"Jud," he moans, but I swallow it with another kiss. His exploring tongue plays with mine.

I have my answer now. Skyler West tastes divine. Like holy perfection.

How am I ever going to kiss another guy without thinking how much they don't taste like Sky?

Fine, I'll become a monk.

My sudden laugh breaks us apart.

"Okay, I know for a fact my kissing game is on point, so what's funny?" he asks.

I shake my head. "You don't want to know. Also, who says you can stop kissing me?"

When I think we can't get any closer than we are, Sky picks me up so I end up with my legs around his waist.

"Oh, you have good ideas," I say and go back to kissing him.

He's walking us somewhere, but I don't care. As long as he avoids stepping on my lucky rock, that's all that matters.

Yeah, that rock I lost my footing on? That's my all-time favorite rock. I'll need to remember to take it home with me.

Sky lowers us down on the big tree log but leaves me straddling him, and I'm not complaining.

He runs his teeth down my jaw, sucking the skin on my neck.

Please mark me. Fucking, please mark me.

"You taste so fucking good, Jud."

Sky's warm hands roam under my clothes, and I need more. I need him all over me.

I unzip my jacket and throw it on the ground, but when I go to unzip Sky's, he puts his hands on mine.

There's no time to wonder if this is already coming to an end because he removes his jacket and drapes it over the log behind me before pushing me back so I'm lying down.

I loosen my legs from around his waist as he covers my body with his. My dick is straining against my jeans, and I can't help bucking against him when he pushes my sweater up and sucks on my nipples one at a time until I'm a blubbering, moaning mess.

"You're so fucking sexy, Jud. One day you're gonna tell all about this ink on your body."

"Yes."

He comes up again, nipping at my lips.

"Can I taste you?" he asks.

"Please." My voice is raspy and needy.

Sky gives me one more kiss, and then his hands are busy opening the fly of my jeans. He strokes my cock over my boxer shorts, and the fabric rubbing against my erection borders on painful.

He lowers the elastic band over my cock, but the relief of being set free is only momentary because Sky takes it in his mouth until my cockhead hits his throat, and I let out a moan that I'm pretty sure people in Burlington can hear.

"Fuck…Sky…your mouth…Jesus…"

I can't even hold my head up to watch him because it feels so good. He wraps his hand around the base of my cock to stop me from coming, and then his mouth is on my balls.

Two months ago, I didn't even know Sky was gay, and now

he's fucking taking the gay crown, the scepter, the whole fucking kingdom.

I'm desperately trying to come and also *not* come because I don't want this to ever end. I want to feel Sky's strong hands exploring my body as if it's his to own.

"Please don't stop," I shout when I no longer feel his touch.

I look up, and the intensity of Sky's gaze is matched by how I feel. He undoes the buttons on his jeans and takes himself out.

He's...fuck, even his dick is perfect. My mouth waters at the sight of his big hand wrapped around his shaft. I ignore my own cock and sit up, but I can't just watch. I need to taste him.

Keeping my eyes on his, I get up from the log and kneel in front of him before I lower my head down until I can no longer keep eye contact. I wrap my hand over his and take his crown in my mouth.

His sweet and salty taste hits my tongue, and I suck, wanting to taste more of his flavor. Sky's other hand lands on my head to keep me there.

I remove my hand, and he gets the message, letting me suck on his crown while he teases his shaft just the way he likes.

We're in the middle of an orchard, wide open for anyone to see. Not that anyone would come this way, we're far away enough from the farm. But being out here like this, doing something we've never done before, feels forbidden and so goddamn erotic.

"Jud, I'm close."

My chest expands with the sound of Sky's struggling voice.

I release his cock and stand up, taking my previous position straddling him, and then I claim his mouth again.

Sky opens for me, and I take everything I can. I taste him, lick him, bite him, and then gasp when he wraps his hand around both of our cocks. With his other arm, he brings me closer to him.

"Fuck, I never knew it could be this good," he says.

I laugh, but it's choked because his big, strong hand is doing things to me. This would only be better if his cock was inside me, but feeling his steel-hard flesh against me is a close second.

"You don't come across like a virgin damsel, so I'm going to take that as a compliment," I joke.

Sweat runs down my back as I thrust into Sky's hand.

"Do it, Jud. Take your pleasure, take everything."

"Sky…" I groan, finally letting go as my orgasm takes over and I have no choice but to ride it.

Sky's orgasm follows mine, and even though he's not inside me and I'm not inside him, I still feel every vibration coming from his big, strong body.

The way his body shakes against mine. The way he holds me tight in his grip. Fuck, it's doing things to my heart that could prove to be fatal.

I have my face buried in the crook of his neck. We're both breathing heavily, and he still hasn't let go of our cocks. If he doesn't, there's a good chance I'll be ready to go again soon. *That's* how much his touch affects me.

Fuck. How will I ever go back to normal?

My hand will never be good enough. Someone else's mouth will never be good enough.

"Jud…"

Sky leans back, and his eyes are full of emotion.

I don't want to think about this. It was good when we were feeling. Just feeling.

I kiss him, and he languidly melts into my kiss. My cock has gone soft, and it feels weird having it out, but I much prefer focusing on Sky's amazing mouth.

We finally part again. His hand, the one that isn't covered in cum, comes around to cradle my face.

His thumb caresses my cheek. I can already feel the tingle in my skin from his short scruff.

"God, I've been waiting for this moment for ten fucking years, Jud."

18

SKYLER

"What?" Jud asks, pulling back so quickly that he almost falls off the fallen log.

What is he doing?

I stand up and tuck myself back in, using my T-shirt to clean my hands, taking it off when I'm done. Thank goodness I decided to put it on under my sweater this morning, or I'd need to find some tree leaf or something.

"What's the matter?" I ask. Jud is looking at me like I've offended him. I try to get closer, but he steps away.

"Jud."

"No, don't touch me." His voice is loud enough for some birds to take flight from nearby trees. He seems startled but manages to catch himself and starts walking back to the bike.

"What did I do?" I call after him.

"Can we go back?" he asks. "This was nice, but—"

"Nice? This...was nice?" I interrupt.

Is he upset? Why is he upset? I should be the one who's upset.

"What do you want me to say, Sky? You give good head? You have magical hands? I think you can agree with me that it *was* nice."

I don't know why I expected anything different from this.

These are words I've heard many times from hookups, but from Jud's mouth, they make it sound like what we just did was dirty.

Is it me? Has he regretted it already because it's me?

"You know what, Jud? Fuck you."

"What do you want from me?" he shouts, turning around and almost tripping over the same stone he stepped on earlier.

"I want you to tell me what's wrong. I want you to tell me you didn't feel what just happened. And I want you to tell me why you left ten years ago." By the time I finish, I'm shouting as loud as he is. I'm glad we're far enough away from the farm that no one will hear us.

"We're back to that then. You couldn't leave it alone, could you?"

Jud runs his hands through his hair, messing it up, and I hate myself for thinking even now that he looks so beautiful. Even when he's angry. Even when I'm angry?

Why are we so fucking angry?

I take a deep, calming breath.

"Why did you run away, Jud?"

"I don't want to talk about it."

"Why?"

Fuck, I wanted to have this conversation another time. I wanted to wait for the right time to ask him the question that's been burning in my mind all these years.

It's too late now. I've opened the box, and now the lid won't fit until I have answers.

"Because I don't want to hear you say it again," he says, and I swear I see his eyes get shiny before he turns the other way.

"Say what?" I step a little closer, but I don't touch him.

"How boring I am, how ugly and fat. I heard you say it once, and I don't want to look at your face as you deny a lifetime of friendship. As you take away all my beautiful memories and burn them into dust with those hateful words. I don't want to look into your eyes as you once again invalidate my entire fucking life."

"What are you talking about? I would never—"

"Stop." He turns around and stares into my eyes.

Tears stream down his beautiful face.

"I was there the night of our graduation party," he says.

"I know, we went together." That night is imprinted in my memory. Every single second.

"We all went to McKenzie Park. You picked a spot for us because it wasn't far from where some guys had all the drinks we weren't supposed to have, but there was a path to the forest right behind us."

I nod. I remember being so scared the police would come, and we'd be in trouble with our parents. Running into the forest would give us a head start, and we'd played there enough growing up that I knew we'd find the way back to Jud's place.

"I needed to pee, so I left to find a tree or bush. When I came back, I thought it would be funny to jump out and scare the shit out of you. But you weren't on your own."

"Blake." Just saying his name brings back the memories. What he asked me…what I told him…and then I know. With sickening clarity, I remember the awful and untrue words I said.

Fuck. Fuck.

This is like one of those movie moments when you're about to die and you see your life flash in front of your eyes. Except, what I see isn't my life. What I see is that one moment that cost me the boy I'm pretty sure I was in love with all those years ago.

"How much did you hear?" I ask.

"Everything."

"Jud."

He raises his hands between us. "No, Sky. It took me a long time to process and get over it. I moved to the other side of the world to run away from the hurt you caused. Think of a broken teenager who just had his life turned inside out, moving on his own across the world. You know how hard that was? I was so alone. But eventually, it got better. I made friends and grew up into this current mess."

He lets out a choked laugh at his own self-deprecating comment.

"Why did you have to go so far?"

"I thought I was running away from you and how you made me feel, away from our fake friendship. But after a while, I realized that it wasn't you that I was running from. It was me. All the things you said were true, so I needed to go somewhere I could hide until I was strong enough to reinvent myself."

I reach over to him, and this time he lets me touch him. I raise the sleeve of his sweater.

"Your tattoos. Losing the weight," I whisper.

He nods.

My knees aren't strong enough to hold me anymore, and I fall onto the ground. No wonder he hated me from the moment we saw each other at the bar.

"I'm so sorry, Jud. I'm so sorry."

To my surprise, Jud sits in front of me cross-legged. He's not crying anymore. It's as if now that his truth has come out, he's finally free.

"Why did you say those things, Sky? I understand feeling that way. But why did you say them?"

I guess it's time for me to tell my truth.

19

JUDSON

I always knew that if I ever had this conversation with Sky, it would hurt. I just never imagined how much. Or that it would be right after shared orgasms. Or that some perverted part of my brain still hoped that I'd misunderstood what he said that night.

Sky keeps his eyes on the ground between us.

"I was so happy when you told me you were gay," he says.

Huh? "Why?"

"Because it meant things wouldn't change for us. If you weren't interested in girls, I wouldn't lose you."

"You realize I could have chased boys, right?"

He smiles, but it doesn't reach his eyes.

"I didn't think of that at the time. I just thought that as long as we were friends and spent all our time together that you wouldn't need anyone else."

"Sky, are you trying to say...did you...back then?"

He nods, and I'm floored. If I wasn't already on the ground, I would be falling. My mind tries to put all the pieces in the right place, but it's just too confusing.

"I always felt good around you. You understood me, Jud. When everyone at school started dating, I figured I had to do it too, even though I didn't feel like asking any girls out. It took me a long time to figure out why. Well, it took me two failed attempts at dating girls to figure out why."

My heart is beating so fast, I put my hand to my chest to calm it down.

"I decided that I was going to tell you how I felt the night of the graduation party. I don't know why that night in particular, but it was the end of school and the start of the last summer before college. It felt right. I came out to my parents before the party. You won't be surprised to know it wasn't news to them. Miles, of course, teased me to death, saying we were going to get married at eighteen and be like those weird teenage couples from reality TV shows."

Sky looks up at me, and I feel that I'm seeing him for the first time in a very long time.

When I thought I saw him at the bar, I hadn't.

When I thought I saw him on the pavement outside Noah's house, I hadn't.

Maybe I almost saw him that night in Fairlington, but I didn't.

Even as we shared something so intimate moments ago, I still didn't see him.

But I see him now.

"I'm sorry I said those things to Blake. I panicked. He came to me, asking if you were seeing someone. I wanted to say, *me, you were with me*, but I wanted to come out to you first, so I said no. He just wanted to hook up with you. He said he thought you were cute, but just to mess around with because his parents would never accept him if they knew he was with a guy. I couldn't stand the thought that you'd do all those first-time things with someone who didn't care for you as much as I did. I wanted those first-time things for us." He looks down again. "So, I told him you were boring, ugly, and fat. I was stupid and thought saying those things would make him back off, which it did, so I don't regret saying it because if he really liked you, what I said wouldn't have mattered. And you deserved someone who wasn't hiding, who didn't just use you and keep you a secret...I waited for you all night."

"But I'd left."

He nods. "It took me a few days to try to see you because we had some issues with the cows. When I finally went to your place and your mom told me you'd left, I was heartbroken. She said you'd be back soon, and we'd have a chance to make up."

"But I didn't come back."

"You did eventually." This time Sky's smile reaches his eyes. "And it gave me time to grow into this irresistible hunk."

I laugh when he flexes his arms.

"And look at you, Mister Tattooed Bad-Boy Chef."

"You don't hate me," I say.

"No."

"How come?"

"Because I like you too much, Judson Hale. I like you too damn much to feel anything else."

I close my hands over Sky's, and he turns his palms up to touch mine. We don't say anything for a while. It's just the sounds of the birds around us, the sun high in the sky, and the slightly damp soil beneath us.

"Why did you believe it so easily?" Sky asks. "We were friends since the day we were born. Why was my lie so easy to believe?"

As I think about it, more memories come to me. Things I'd heard, things I'd seen, and my own fears mixed in. We never stood a chance.

Would I have ended up pushing Sky away because I was so afraid I wasn't good enough?

"You had a growth spurt senior year, and I noticed everyone was suddenly watching you. I'd hear people in the locker rooms or on the way to class. *What is Skyler doing with that fat loser? Do you think he'll come to my birthday party without Judson? Skyler is so hot, shame he has a bad smell hanging around him all the time. He must be gay. It's the only explanation.*"

"Jud, all those things were lies. All those people had no idea how I felt. They were so wrong because you were the sun. I orbited around you like a planet, and they weren't even space dust. They were nothing, and you were everything. I'm so sorry they made you feel otherwise."

I sigh. "Stop saying nice stuff because you're making me want to kiss you."

"Good." Sky leans forward, closing the small distance between us, and presses his lips against mine.

Our kiss is tender, like a long-due apology. We both did wrong by each other, but we both lived the consequences. So much time has passed. Does the past still matter?

I deepen the kiss, running my tongue over his lips and enjoying when he moans and opens his mouth to let me taste him. I don't know what kissing Sky would have been like at eighteen, but at twenty-eight? It's fucking mind-blowing.

Unfortunately, my belly rumbles and Sky breaks off the kiss. The smile on his face could win awards if there was such a thing.

"Is my mouth making you hungry?" he jokes.

"Yes, for more. Come here."

I pull him back to me, but he puts his hand between our mouths. I lick it and kiss it, loving how his eyes go dark.

"Let's eat whatever snack my mom prepared for us. You know if we don't eat it all and then show up hungry for dinner, we'll be in trouble."

I chuckle, remembering the times we'd been in trouble with our moms for getting so lost playing outside that we forgot our snacks. There's probably a family of raccoons out there in Burlington that was exclusively fed by us for years.

We stand up, shaking off the soil from our clothes, and walk toward the bike where Sky left the bag hanging from the handlebar.

Sky opens the bag and starts laughing.

"What's funny?"

"How hungry are you?" he asks.

"I could eat. Why?"

He comes closer for another drugging kiss. Fuck, I could get used to this.

"Will my kisses be enough?" he whispers against my mouth.

"Well, they're certainly distracting. What were we talking about again?"

He puts his hand inside the bag and pulls out two apples.

"I guess she doesn't want us to lose track of time," I say.

"She underestimates how long I've dreamed about having you in my arms. With this apple and the coffee I had earlier, I think I have enough hydration to keep you here for the next three days."

I wrap my arms around his waist and lean my head on his chest. "But how about energy? You need energy for the stuff I have in mind for you."

He kisses my head and laughs. "You also underestimate how long I've wanted you, Jud."

I look up to give him another kiss.

"Have you always been such a smooth talker?"

"Only for the things I really want."

"And you want me?"

"I do."

20

SKYLER

"Put this on," Jud says, waving a sleep mask in front of me.

I raise a brow. "Here. In your mother's kitchen?"

"Put it on."

God, he's sexy when he's bossy.

"Okay, but if someone walks in, you're doing the explaining."

He laughs.

Since the day at the orchard, we haven't spent as much time together as I would like. After dinner with my parents, my dad announced that he let go of the extra help I hired.

That swiftly put to bed my plan to invite Jud to meet me at the cabin that night because we had an early morning the next day.

The only time I was able to spend with him was when, after collecting a bag of vegetables from my mom, he came with me to Montpelier, Colebury, and Tuxbury to deliver syrup to the shops that stock Maple Sky.

We still made the best of our time together and went for a walk after each delivery and just talked. And we made out...a lot. Who knew my truck would be such a perfect location to make out?

Since he's off work today, he invited me to come to his place so I can sample his food.

After a full day at the farm, which included chasing Florrie once again, being fed by Jud while wearing a blindfold is my idea of heaven. If only we were naked and *not* in his mom's kitchen.

"Okay, I'm going to put some food in front of your nose. Smell it," he says.

I feel the warmth and steam from whatever he puts in front of my nose. It smells creamy and sweet at the same time.

"Now, open your mouth."

I do, and I immediately identify the asparagus and pasta in a creamy sauce.

"Why is it sweet? Did you put maple syrup in it?" I ask as all the flavors mix in my mouth. It's delicious.

"Yeah, a little bit. The nutmeg really brings out the flavors and gives it an extra layer, don't you think?"

I nod.

"Here's the next one," he says, and after smelling the delicious meat, I realize it's veal in a tomato sauce, which he follows with a maple-glazed roast potato.

"God, this is so good. Where do I sign up to have this for the rest of my life?"

"At the registry office, dear."

I cough when I hear Jud's mom's voice and then remove the blindfold.

It doesn't take long for my eyes to adjust to the brightness of the kitchen lights. Jud is hiding his face behind his hands while his mom stares at us with a smile.

When I say smile...I mean challenge.

"Do you want to try the food, Mom?" Jud asks.

One by one, all the members of the Hale family come into the kitchen and try Jud's food, which is a great success. Not that I had any doubts about Jud's talent in the kitchen. After all, he is his mother's son.

After the feast, they leave us to discuss the menu. We told both our families about the show as soon as we wrapped our minds around the fact that we would be on TV. After all, they will be included in the *fly-on-the-wall* part of the filming.

We clean everything and then sit at the kitchen table.

"Your mom's vegetables are really good. We may still need to source some stuff, but I think we have a good selection already," he says.

I nod. He looks so happy and relaxed after the success of the taste test. I want to reach out and kiss him, but his family could walk back into the kitchen any moment.

The way he looks at me tells me he's thinking the same.

"Follow me," he says, standing up.

He peeks through to the den and looks satisfied with whatever he sees, then he nods for me to follow him outside.

As soon as I see where he's headed, I smile.

His house leads onto a field at the back. When we were kids, we carved out a path in the corner of the tall hedge surrounding the backyard so we could hang out of sight from his parents.

Not that we ever did anything that required any kind of secrecy. Mostly we just talked about our plans to travel the world together after we graduated.

Today, I'm sure our intentions are a lot less innocent.

As soon as we're through the hedge and on the path surrounding the field, Jud wraps his arms around my waist and lifts his head up for a kiss.

I gladly give it to him. We take our time tasting each other. Hands desperately seeking warm skin.

"God, Jud, you drive me insane." I run my teeth down his neck and suck on the skin, knowing I'll leave a mark. It won't be visible under his clothes, but he'll see it. He'll know it's there and exactly who's responsible for it.

"Sky…" His voice has a tinge of desperation, but we can't do anything here. If he's always as loud as he was back at the orchard, then we definitely can't do more than make out.

"I need you at the cabin with me," I say.

"Tonight would be too obvious. I think my mom already suspects there's something between us. I'm working tomorrow night. Day after?"

"It's a date." I claim his mouth again before I force myself to let go.

The next day is one of those days that make it so easy to forget that, for endless months, Vermont has more shades of gray than a paint swatch.

The sky is blue, with a few white clouds scattered around, the flower beds on Church Street are blooming, and there's a nice buzz in the air.

Farmer's market day in Burlington is the best day to be out on Church Street. There are so many street entertainers and traders selling their crafts and local foods.

After missing a few weeks because of tapping season, my stall is particularly busy with people wanting to buy this season's maple syrup.

"Hey, Skyler, do you have a box for me?" Celia from Celia's Creemees shouts from her stand.

"Of course. You know I'd never let you down."

"Missed you, gorgeous." She winks, and I wave her off.

The absolute best way to end the day at the market is with one of her delicious maple-and-vanilla flavored creemees, and I don't plan to break that tradition.

Celia wants me to be her sole supplier of maple syrup, but until I can increase my production, I can't take her offer.

I still have sixty percent of my forest untapped. My business does well on the current production, but I like having room for expansion.

"Should I be jealous?"

I turn around to see Jud standing an arm's distance away. I want to reach out and pull him even closer, but the crew from the show will turn up any moment with cameras, and we'd agreed that we didn't want our private life to play out on the show.

"Of Celia? You do realize she's a hundred years old, right?"

Jud snorts.

"You're a bit early for work, aren't you?" I ask.

He bites his lip and scratches behind his ear, which I now know is his tell. He wants something.

"I changed shifts with Oz," he says. "I'm...not working today."

I laugh, and the part of me that is already so attached to Jud wonders if he feels the same way to the point of changing his shift.

God, I want to kiss him so badly.

"Want to meet me at the cabin at six? I'll let you cook me dinner."

Jud laughs, but I manage to keep a straight face. "What? You don't like my plan?"

"No," he says. "It's a great plan. Tell you what, dinner is on me, dessert is on you, Mister Maple Sky."

My cock thickens. I've never been so glad to be wearing my Maple Sky apron because that's the effect that being around Jud has on me, not to mention that now I'm thinking about all the things I can do with him tonight.

"It's a deal. Now please go before I do something that I shouldn't."

His eyes darken, and a slow smile spreads over his soft lips. "You wouldn't."

"Don't test me."

With slow, practiced moves, he spreads a spoonful of maple cream onto a sample piece of bread and raises it to his mouth. I see his tongue teasing out the maple cream just before he puts the whole piece in his mouth. Then he turns around and leaves.

Fuck, I think I need a creemee to cool me down. But that gives me even more ideas for fun with Jud. Is there anything that doesn't make me horny for Judson Hale?

My answer is a few yards away, where I spot the camera crew approaching.

I put on my best smile and wait for them to make their way to the stall. We were told they'd be like a fly on the wall and to ignore them because they just want to have some shots of us going about our daily lives.

Jud's turn is tomorrow. They're filming at his place while he helps his mom with a cupcake order for a birthday party.

The crew follows me after the market to my parent's farm and gets to see the milk production. We have quite a few calves who are now weaning and being introduced to grass. A lot of what we do at the farm is essential but not nice once you learn more about it. But no one can deny how adorable baby cows are.

As soon as they leave, I tell my mom I'm staying at the cabin. She gives me a strange look when I decline her offer to take some food with me. I tell her not to worry because I froze some of her leftovers from weeks ago, but I don't think she's buying my excuse.

The day I came out, I also told my mom how I felt about Jud. Since then, I haven't made a secret of any of my hookups or brief relationships. She doesn't need to know the details, but I know she cares about me, so I give her as much as I can to show her my heart is well protected.

Except, Jud is here now, and I'm pretty sure both she and Jud's mom already know there's something between us. I stop thinking about it when I approach the cabin and see Jud sitting on the porch steps and playing on his phone, a bag of groceries next to him.

I park the truck and jump out, running straight to him to give him the kiss he should have had earlier today.

"Fuck, Sky. Way to greet a man," he says, adjusting his dick through his jeans.

"You don't approve?"

He pulls me down for another kiss.

"I very much approve, but you stink, and I'm hungry."

"Sorry, babe. Let's go in. I'll get in the shower while you cook."

I don't mean to use the term of endearment, but if it bothers Jud, he doesn't show it. I also can't promise it won't slip out again.

Before I get in the shower, I quickly change my bedsheets. It's been a few weeks since I've slept here regularly, and while they don't smell, I prefer to have my way with Jud in clean bedding.

I'm in full seduction mode. I remembered to turn the heat up on my way out of the kitchen, so after I get out of the shower, I throw on a pair of gray sweatpants, forgoing underwear and a shirt.

I know Jud wants this as much as I do, but showing him exactly how much I want him won't hurt a bit.

There's some kind of classical music coming from the kitchen, and I hear Jud whistling to the melody. When I turn into the kitchen, planning on ogling him from the doorway, my jaw drops.

Touché, Judson. Touché.

I close my eyes and open them again, but I'm not imagining it. I really have Judson Hale in my kitchen, barefoot, wearing just a pair of tight black boxer briefs. He's swaying to the music and stirring something in a pot on the stove.

"Fuck, I think I just came in my pants. You should be illegal," I say.

He turns the stove off and dips his finger in the sauce, licking it before turning around to face me.

I groan and run my hands over my face.

"Dinner's ready," he announces as if this is a situation that happens every day.

Sure, I have a drop-dead gorgeous man, with tattoos for days, almost naked in my kitchen every day. Doesn't everyone?

"What's for dinner?"

"Slow-cooked shredded beef ragu pasta."

"Slow cooked?" Does that mean what I think it means?

Jud must see my thoughts scattered all over my face because he says, "You can stop those ideas right now, hotshot. This beef has been cooking since this morning and the whole thing is ready now." He raises his finger and wiggles it at me. "No shenanigans."

"You should have said that before you decided *that's* what you're wearing to cook in my kitchen." I wave my hand in front of him, and he grabs it, pulling me closer.

"Okay, fine. Some shenanigans allowed."

We kiss, and I taste the sauce on his tongue.

This is the first time I've been this close to Jud without clothes on. His skin feels warm, and I let my hands roam and explore his back, slowly ambling down to his perfectly round and squishable butt.

"We should eat," I say, pulling away with reluctance. His erection against mine is making it too hard to make the right decisions, and I know we need food.

His stomach rumbles.

"Okay, food first. Then dessert," he says.

"What's for dessert?"

"You."

21

JUDSON

How am I supposed to think straight while Sky eats his pasta like he's making love to it?

I stare at my own plate and consider how much more I can have.

Breathe, Jud. Just breathe.

That's my mantra. Ever since I had the ridiculous idea to strip down for Sky, I've been saying it in my head nonstop.

This is one of those moments when I have to actively remember that what my brain thinks it sees when I look down is *not* the reality. My body dysmorphia can be crippling, especially when I'm intimate with someone, but I don't want it to be a thing between Sky and me.

He deserves more than my fucked-up fat-brain.

"Hey." Sky reaches over the table; his hand is on my chin and his thumb making a circular motion. "Where did you go?"

"Nowhere." I stand up and turn him away from the table so I can straddle his legs. "Have you finished dinner yet? Can we have dessert already?"

I take his mouth and suck his tongue until he's moaning and giving it all back, biting my lip and kissing everywhere he can reach on my face, chin, neck.

I move my neck, and he takes the hint, kissing behind my ear, which is an area where I'm really sensitive. The slight tickling gives way to a wave of pleasure that runs down my back and straight to my balls.

"Fuuuck, Sky."

He runs his hands over my chest, tracing my tattoos. When his thumb skates over my nipple, my breath catches, and I have to bite my lip to stop myself from moaning.

"You are so beautiful, Jud. So...unexpected. Being with you is like walking down a road you know so well, but no matter how many times you cross it, you always find something new."

I close my eyes, giving in to his touch and his words. God, why didn't I know that I could crave words?

His tongue flattens out over my nipple, and he sucks it into a sensitive peak before moving to the other one.

There's no hiding how hard we both are. My hips move against him, looking for friction...relief...bliss...

"Sky..." I moan. "More..."

"More what, baby?" He nips at my skin, finding his way to my neck, where I feel him suck a hickey to replace the one he left on me last week, which is an addition to the one he gave me yesterday. I love how he needs to mark me.

Like my tattoos, the hickey won't be visible to anyone, but I'll know it's there. I know he wants it there.

I feel his erection getting harder, and my mouth waters at the thought of his thick, heavy cock against my tongue. I roll my hips to meet his, but it's not enough. The few layers we have between us are too many.

He puts his hands on my butt and stands up, taking me with him.

"Dessert time."

He lays me down on the kitchen island with my ass on the edge.

Yes! Fucking god, yes.

I lean back and squeak as the stone counter cools me down.

Sky removes my underwear, and then I'm gloriously naked like I'm about to be served on a platter.

The sound of a cap makes me look up. I want to watch what Sky is doing, but what he has in his hand isn't what I think it is.

"What are you doing?"

"I told you. I'm having dessert. Now shush and lie back. This is between me and this delectable ass."

I laugh but do as I'm told, and a moment later, I feel the cold drizzle of Maple Sky syrup on my cock and running down my balls toward my hole.

"You better clean that u—FUCK!" I shout as Sky licks and sucks my hole like he hasn't eaten for a year. My body is going haywire, shaking with pleasure.

All the hairs on my skin stand up, and I feel like I'm some kind of conductor for energy that, at some point, will need to find its way out.

Before I know it, my orgasm rips through me like a cannon-ball. There are stars in my eyes, and I think I may actually be dead.

Sky chuckles. "I was not expecting that, but, man, I'll keep on doing it just to see you come so beautifully, Jud."

I can't even talk, so I'm most certainly deceased. Sky doesn't stop licking me though. Maybe he can't stand to waste a drop of his precious syrup, or my cum, because he licks me until I'm all clean and my dick is starting to stir again.

"Is that why you called it Maple Sky? Because I think I'm in heaven."

He pulls my hand until I'm sitting up and facing him, and then he kisses me, slowly, letting me taste the mix of my release and the maple syrup.

"It is now," he says, his laughter rumbling from deep in his chest.

He picks me up again and takes me to his room, past his very comfortable-looking bed, and into the bathroom. I'm very aware that he hasn't come because his very hard dick is poking my ass.

If it wasn't for the lack of prep or the stickiness, I'd be sliding down Sky's waist to get that thing in me.

Sky doesn't put me down until the water in the shower is running warm. I have to say, there are advantages to being with Superman. Lois Lane was a smart girl.

We wash each other until I'm back to full-on hard and ready to go again. Sky runs his teeth down my neck, which results in me bucking into him, our cocks rubbing together between us.

Now that he knows my neck is my Achilles heel, he seems determined to use it against me as much as possible.

"Will you fuck me?" he asks.

"Have you done it before?" I ask before I can catch myself. I don't know why I keep thinking he's inexperienced just because I only recently found out that he's gay. "Sorry, of course, you must have—"

"No. I've never bottomed."

"But...why?"

"Why haven't I bottomed? Or why do I want to?"

"The first."

"Lots of reasons. In case you're wondering, I have a type. Smaller guys with killer attitudes and round butts. If they can make me food, make me laugh, and they're covered in sexy tattoos, then I'm a goner."

I chuckle as he describes me perfectly.

He looks into my eyes. "The truth is, the guys I'm attracted to usually expect me to top. I've been with a few who were happy to switch, but when we got to it, they changed their minds."

"Can't blame them. Have you seen your cock?"

He laughs. "I like yours better, and I'd like it inside me."

I turn the water off and step out of the shower. He grabs two fluffy towels from a shelf, wraps one around his waist, and starts drying me off with the other.

"Sky, you should wait."

"Why?"

"Don't give me something you'll regret one day because you won't be able to take it back."

When he decides I'm dry enough—after making sure my ass, cock, and balls are thoroughly moisture-free, of course—he hangs the towel and dries himself before putting his arms around me again.

"I know what you're doing, Jud. You're trying to protect yourself and me, but this is happening. If not today, then another day because I'm not letting you run away again."

I step away from his hold, but he doesn't let me go completely, lacing our hands together. I hate to bring the mood down, but we can't jump into something just because it feels good. And there's something he needs to know.

"What are we doing, Sky? God, I've wanted you for so long, and even after everything that happened, you still insisted on appearing in my dreams, making me feel good and safe. But we need to be sure of what this is."

"What are you worried about?"

Tell him, Jud. No more secrets.

"Sky, before we do this, I need you to know that I'm not staying here."

Those cute creases on his forehead make an appearance, and I get closer to him again to smooth them out with my thumb.

"What do you mean?" he asks, and I hear the hurt in his voice.

"A friend is expanding his restaurant chain in LA, and he asked me to be his partner. I'm just waiting to get the money from Pierre to buy my share of Spencer's business."

Sky stares into my eyes, and once again, I feel that he sees more than I know is there.

"Is that your dream?" he asks.

"Yes."

"Then why are you doing the show?"

"Because that's your dream, and I want to help you get what you want. If we win, you're bypassing a load of costly steps toward having your own store. You can use the money you saved to hire someone to look after the store for you so you can still help your parents out at the farm until Miles comes back."

Sky lets out a breath.

"God, Jud. How am I supposed to let you go when you say stuff like that?"

"I'm sorry."

"Does it really have to end?"

What does he mean?

Does he want to have a long-distance relationship? It'll never work.

He puts his hands on my face, so I look into his eyes again. "Come back to me, baby. Let's not think about this now. Let's just do what makes us feel good, okay?"

"I can do that." I can certainly do that.

He's dry enough for me, so I hang his towel next to mine, ignoring how my heart beats a little faster, seeing them both up there as if that's how it's meant to be. I pull him by the hand and lead him to his bed.

"You've had your dessert, but I haven't had mine," I say. "Although, to be fair, I liked how your dessert came out in the end. So this is how it's going to go..."

"Oh, bossy Jud. Have I told you how much I like it when you're bossy?" he says, slapping my ass.

I throw myself on the bed and pull him down on top of me.

He slams his hungry mouth onto mine, and I welcome it. I'll end up with beard rash and bruised lips, but I want it all. Being consumed by Sky like this is the absolute best feeling in the world.

"God, I love how big you are. So strong, solid. Pin me down," I beg.

He takes my hands and pins them above my head, holding them with one hand while the other runs slowly down my body.

I squirm when his fingers tickle my sides.

"I love this. That you're still ticklish. God, you got me so hard that day on the sidewalk in Fairlington," he says into my mouth.

"Hmm..."

I raise my hips, but he raises his too, the fucker.

"Patience, baby. You'd think you haven't had an orgasm today." He's nipping at my neck again, and I swear I'll kill him if I have visible marks in the morning.

"Stop being so fucking sexy, and I'll stop coming in three-point-two seconds," I groan.

His hand finally moves where I want it to, and just like at the orchard, he grips us both. The weight of his body, the tight grip from his hand, and the words he's whispering in my ear are enough to bring me to the brink of ultimate pleasure.

"I'm so close, baby. Are you going to let go too?" he asks.

"Uh huh."

I open my eyes, and he's right there, looking back at me. A little bead of sweat runs down his forehead, and I just want to lick it.

My pleasure is there under the surface but not quite attainable. Sky's moves become more erratic, and I feel like he's pressing me flat against the mattress. He comes with a groan, his hips jerking until he's spent.

He releases my hands, and I reach down for my still-hard dick.

"Sky...I need..." I beg. I don't even know what I'm begging for. As far as I know, he doesn't even know his name right now. He's like a giant noodle on top of me.

But he's not quite dead yet, and he knows I haven't come because he reaches down between my legs and finds my crease.

As soon as I feel his finger putting pressure on my hole to seek entrance, that's it. That is all I needed. The tiny trigger that pushes me over to the next level.

Sky kisses me again as I come down from my orgasm. Damn, sex with him is so good.

That's my second to last thought before I fall asleep. My last thought is that I hope he's not expecting me to go home now because I'm not leaving his comfy bed and his warm body for anything but a life-or-death emergency.

22

SKYLER

Waking up with Jud fast asleep and snoring lightly against me has to be the best thing in the world.

His head is on my chest, his leg is draped over mine, and his arm is around my waist. Every so often, his fingers twitch as if he's dreaming, and he lets out these cute little whimpers.

I think about his refusal to top me last night. I understand why he doesn't want to do it, so I need to find a way to explain to him how I feel about it.

All of my firsts should have belonged to him.

He should have been my first kiss with a boy, first hand job, first blowjob, first everything. I can't give him those, but I can let him be the first man to top me. To be inside my body in a way no one has ever been.

His eventual move to LA doesn't change that.

I don't want to think too much about that particular piece of news because I already know I won't be able to let him go. I'll do the long-distance thing if I need to, but hopefully, by the time he's ready to leave, he'll have had a taste of life with me and won't want to go.

A guy can dream, right?

He twitches, and then his body locks as he stretches like a cat before letting out a contented sigh and looking up at me like he really did get the cream.

I put my previous thought aside because, right now, all I want to do is kiss the beautiful man in my arms.

"Morning," he says.

"Morning, beautiful."

Our lips meet as if they've been waking up to each other for years.

"I'm sorry I fell asleep on you yesterday, but it's all your fault, so…" he says.

"Oh really? How so?"

He raises one finger. "Bone-melting orgasms—plural." And then another. "Pasta dinner."

"Hey, I was only responsible for dessert. Dinner was on you."

He sighs. "Fine." He rests his chin on my chest, but his eyes don't meet mine. "Thank you for not kicking me out. I really shouldn't have fallen asleep like that."

I narrow my eyes, and I'm glad he's not looking at me because he'd probably misinterpret my current expression.

"Jud, you're not a random hookup. For the record, I've never brought anyone here. This is my home, and there's no space for strangers here. In case you haven't noticed, you're anything but a stranger. You falling asleep saved me from having to ask you and panicking over whether you'd say yes or no. And by the way, if you want a repeat tonight, just be here at the same time."

He smiles and looks at me again, stretching up for a kiss.

"I'm working tonight. Raincheck?"

"Absolutely."

"I have an idea for the restaurant. I was going to tell you yesterday, but…maple syrup." He shrugs.

"Okay."

"Remember we talked about serving the food we grew up with but with a little extra? More finesse, new flavors, or presented in a new way? I'm thinking maybe we could give the diners a recipe card so they can replicate the dish at home."

"But won't that mean people will stop coming to the restaurant? Why would they come if they can make the same food at home?"

Jud's eyes light up, and he almost hums with excitement.

"I've worked in restaurants for years, and the best part of being in the kitchen is when we change the menu completely because we can experiment with new combinations of flavors, cuisines, and work on giving our diners the best experience. We want them to come to us every few months to check out the new menu. But Burlington isn't Paris. You want people to come to the restaurant every week. Like the kind of family tradition you grew up with. So that, years from now, people will say, *remember when we used to go to Maple Sky on Tuesdays?*"

I can't stop touching Jud, but he's so animated, I don't think he's paying attention to my roaming hands, even as they get closer to his cute ass.

"Anyway, for people to come every week you have to change the menu more often, maybe once a month or every six weeks. It's not easy, and it requires a lot of planning. When I was at culinary school, we were taught how to create a menu that uses the same ingredients because it's more cost-effective, and it allows you to do more of some dishes without running out or having a lot of waste. Wouldn't you want to go to Maple Sky every week to try a new dish and take home a recipe card?"

He sits up suddenly. "I have another idea. What if people could bring a sample of the food they made using the cards? The chef would try it and score it, and once a week, the home cook with the best attempt would get a meal on the house."

"You want to build a community." It dawns on me. I'm not sure it's what Jud had planned, but that's the result. And I get it. The whole time he was in Europe, he didn't have his family or friends, his community. "I think it's a beautiful idea, baby."

He lies back down on my chest, and everything is silent again as it was when he was asleep. My heart feels like it's traveled up to my throat and is lodged there.

I like this, and I don't want him to leave. I don't want him to go make his amazing food for people in LA. I want him here with me, running Maple Sky, which, in a weird roundabout way, is *our* dream.

He sits up with a jolt.

"Oh, crap, I have to run. The film crew is going to turn up at my place any time now, and I'm not sure I want to let my mom loose on them."

He runs to the living room, where he left his clothes, and minutes later, he's on his way out after letting me kiss him stupid.

I get myself ready and make my way to the farm. I think that if I stay there tonight, I might sneak out to the bar and see Jud.

Shortly after arriving at the farm, I realize there's no chance of that happening tonight because my dad has an accident out in the field and ends up spraining his wrist.

After a trip to the hospital, we're late on all the farm jobs, and I'm the only one around to do them.

"Hey, honey," my mom says, leaning against the gate.

I'm collecting cow manure to use as compost on my mom's garden. My back's killing me, and I want to be anywhere else but here.

"Hey, Ma. How's he doing? Painkillers working yet?"

"Yeah. He's going to be a pain in the ass for the next few weeks, but he's been a pain in my ass for the last thirty years, so I can't see what's different."

"Have you spoken to Miles?"

She tucks a loose strand of hair behind her ear. So no, she hasn't told him, because she doesn't want to worry him.

I can't blame her. Miles has a whole life of this crap ahead of him. He doesn't need to start it a day earlier. He'd drop everything to come back, and he's worked too hard on his degree to give it all up now.

"I was thinking we should see if Francis is still looking for work. I knew we shouldn't have let him go, but your dad wouldn't listen. You have the show coming up, and with your dad like this..."

She's right. "How's the account?"

"We can't afford him right now, but we're waiting for a couple of payments from milk buyers, so I think we'll manage."

"Do you mind calling Francis? And if those payments don't come through, you tell me so I can chase them."

"Okay, honey. I'll go back in to hit your dad with a stick for being silly and hurting himself, and I suppose I'll get dinner started too."

Everything might be going to shit, but at least the Wests never lose their sense of humor.

23

JUDSON

I'm talking to a customer about the differences between French and Californian red wine when I see Sky approach the bar.

Molly gives me a look that says she's noticed how Sky has started to come here on his own, sitting at the bar just so he can see me.

I try to give her a casual shrug, but I don't think I'm fooling anyone.

Word has come out about the show, and everyone is talking about it. The mayor is the new town hero for having such a great idea, and there are a ton of rumors about what the old hostel will turn out to be in the end.

Of course, no one's seen it yet because the boards covering the windows were soon replaced with bigger boards covering the entire space in front of the hostel.

Curiosity is a powerful marketing strategy, so as soon as booking opened for the restaurant, the website crashed under the weight of all the traffic from people wanting to know who the contestants are and to book a place for their week.

I approach Sky, trying my best to look unaffected by how great he looks in his long-sleeve baseball T-shirt. At the best of times,

Sky looks delectable, but when he's looking all casual hunky, I swear my knees go a little weak.

"Hey, have I seen you here before, sir?" I joke.

He smiles, but then he looks around and his face goes a bit more serious.

"Can we talk? Do you have a break coming up?"

"I've had my break, but I can take five, hold on."

Rainn was the last to have a break, and he's back now, so I check with Tanner to see if he minds me taking a few minutes. He grunts his reply but points to the function room.

As far as I can tell, we haven't had any functions booked because we've been using it as surplus storage for wine. I'm really proud to see that my wine sessions with the team have increased sales.

I'm so glad the function room doors don't have any glass in them because as soon as we're inside the room, Sky closes the doors and pushes me against them, claiming my mouth.

My need for him ramps up, and I start humping the leg he eased between my thighs to keep me in place. He releases my mouth to go for the kill.

Why did I ever let him know how much I love when he touches my neck? Fuck, I think I could come from him breathing on it alone.

"Sky…" I groan.

"One minute."

I chuckle. "There are cameras in here."

He releases my neck so quickly, I wonder if he sprained his. "No way."

My eyes dart up to the camera in the corner, and he follows my line of sight.

"Fuck." He adjusts his erection, and I do the same as he puts a little distance between us.

"It's okay. It's unlikely anyone's going to watch the tape when there isn't a function."

He raises a brow. "Have you met your colleagues? They're probably huddled up watching us with popcorn in hand."

I snort. "Did you need something? Or did you just have this random primal need to maul me at work? For the record, I don't mind if it's the second."

He laughs. "My need to maul you is anything but random. It's more like a constant thing that gnaws at me until I break my resolve and drive the distance from the farm to Burlington just so I can smell your aftershave."

"Oh, is that what you were doing? Smelling my aftershave? I could have mistaken it for giving me a fresh hickey in place of the one that *just* healed."

He smiles at me in that way I can't resist, and cameras be damned, I go in for another kiss.

This time it's Sky who breaks it.

"I have some news. I got a call earlier from the production team to say that they've had to bump everyone up because someone in the team who's starting off the show was in an accident."

"Oh my gosh, are they okay?"

"Yeah, it wasn't serious, but it shook the team up, and because they're not local, they need to get a new van."

I walk around the middle of the room, which is clear of all furniture at the moment. Each team opens on a Sunday and closes on the following Sunday, giving the next team five days to get their kitchen up and running, as well as any decor changes they may have requested. Which means…

"Fuck. Are they fucking kidding us?" I run my hand through my hair, pulling it tight. "What are we going to do? We have three days to contact all of our suppliers and get them to deliver two weeks early. The recipe cards haven't arrived from the production team because they're not supposed to be ready for another two freaking weeks."

Sky comes over and takes my hands in his. "Hey…hey…look

at me. We're gonna make this happen, okay? The production team will help us with what they can, right? They've been cool so far."

He's right. Apart from the constant questions about whether Sky and I are a couple or not and incessantly trying to catch us in an intimate moment, they've been pretty good.

"Okay, I'll ask Tanner to move my shifts. Can I go home with you tonight? I don't think I'll be able to settle on my own." I hate to ask the question, but I'm too wound up to care.

"I was counting on it. Now, let's go back before you get in trouble."

My face gives me away when we leave the room because Molly looks at me and then Sky. As soon as I'm behind the bar, she pulls me to the staff area.

"Are you okay? Is everything okay between you and Skyler?"

"Yeah, why wouldn't it be?"

She shrugs. "I don't know. New relationships are tough—"

"Wait…what?"

"Oh, stop pretending. You're not the first, or even the second, guy here to shack up with a customer."

"I'm not…" I start, but she gives me a look that shuts me up.

"Anyway, what's wrong?"

I give Molly a brief summary, and she declares a staff meeting at the end of the shift.

Tanner raises a brow but doesn't shut her down.

Sky spends most of the rest of my shift, sitting at the bar and nursing a cider while snaking on a bowl of chips I gave him. I am most definitely considering future forms of stress relief, and I can't have him drunk for it.

He also seems to disappear outside a few times, and every time he comes back, he looks a lot happier.

As soon as we close the bar and start cleaning, Molly takes it upon herself to gather the troops. It's crazy how much that girl is a natural on stage.

"I spoke to a few suppliers, and we're going to start getting deliveries tomorrow morning," Sky says. "But the production team has an issue with their printers and can't get the menus to us in time."

"Are we supposed to sing the menu to the diners?" I ask, trying to keep my temper in check as I clean the tables.

"I volunteer as a tribute," Molly says, raising her hand.

Even in my currently stressed state, I consider the merits of that. Molly does have a beautiful voice.

"How about Auden?" Rainn says.

"Who's Auden?" I ask.

"He used to work here, but now he runs Imprescott Designs with his boyfriend, Carter. They're a bit upmarket, but they're local, and the advertising will be good for their business."

"Anyone up for picking up Judson's shifts?" Tanner asks.

A few hands raise.

"Okay, now that's arranged, Judson and Skyler, go home," Tanner says.

"But—" I start, but he gives me a do-not-argue stare.

I'm completely floored at everyone's support. "Thank you. You have no idea how much this means to us," I say.

"Yeah, we do," Rainn says. "And don't think you're off the hook. We expect a free five-course meal when you win that show. We even have a kitchen and a function room right here. Right, boss?"

"After I bleach my eyes, yes," Tanner mutters under his breath, but with the bar music turned off, I can hear him, and so can everyone else.

There's a round of cheers while I'm sure I evaporate from how hot I feel.

Sky takes my hand and leads me behind the bar, stopping only when he realizes he has no clue where the exit is.

I lead him out of the bar through the loading bay door and around the building to the main road.

"By the way, you're driving. I walked here."

"How were you planning on getting home?" he asks, looking a

little worried, but then he finds his answer. He pinches my butt, and I squeak. "Am I that sure of a thing?"

"You mean, was I *sure* you were going to turn up? No. Am I *sure* you're dying to get your tongue all over my ass? Hell yeah."

"You cocky bastard. Just wait until I get you in my bed."

"Promises, promises."

24

SKYLER

"Skyler, how do you feel?" Yolanda, the show's presenter, asks.

"Have you ever seen a cow give birth?"

She stares at me with a horrified face, and I chuckle.

"It's a long process, and there isn't much you can do about it other than controlling the mother's environment, make sure she's not stressed, and that she's comfortable. When it finally happens, it's the most wonderful thing. It's mother nature at its best.""Are you," she coughs, "are you comparing the opening of your restaurant to a cow giving birth?"

"Like I said. It's magical. You should see it one day. But to answer your question, the reason you're talking to me right now rather than standing in the kitchen with the camera crew is because that's where the magic happens. We created a good menu filled with locally sourced foods, and right now, Judson and the team of cooks are all working hard to get it ready for our first diners."

"Well, I wish you both all the luck this week."

"Thank you."

The cameraman gives us a sign that he's no longer recording, and I let out a sigh.

"You did well. The viewers are going to love you both," she says.

"Thanks…um, I better go check on Jud."

She gives the cameraman a nod to follow her outside.

The boards in front of the restaurant were taken down yesterday to reveal the wooden plaque with the name of the restaurant. We're calling ours Maple Sky, which Jud insisted on.

He says it's the perfect name both for my brand and for the restaurant. I want the world to know there's something of Jud in it, too, but he keeps on saying this is my business.

I've parked *that* conversation until after the show because we're both too stressed to talk about the fact that we've been basically seeing each other every day, sleeping together at night, and doing all the things that make this very much a relationship.

I check in with the waiters, who are all busy making the final adjustments and adding the fresh flowers that were delivered this morning to the tables.

With everything ready at the front, I go see my man in the kitchen.

The camera crew left, but there are cameras set up all over the kitchen, so I know I can't touch him like I wish I could. I'm expecting to see a stressed-out Jud, but when I go through the double doors, all I hear is laughter.

Jud's smile as he sees me is unmistakable. You'd have to be blind or stupid not to see how we feel about each other.

"The memo I got was that I was required to be stressed today," I joke.

"You must not have gotten the updated one," Jud says. "From now until we close the restaurant next Sunday, only jokes are allowed in this kitchen."

"What day do eggs hate the most?" asks the sous chef. "Fry Day."

"Hear this one," the other assistant says. "What did the host of Top Chef say to the contestants?"

And they all reply, "Lettuce begin."

"Don't worry," Jud says. "Their jokes are terrible, but they know how to cook."

"Damn right," they all chime in.

I nudge Jud to follow me, and he nods back.

"Why did the chef have to stop cooking? He ran out of thyme," he says as his parting contribution.

"I want to show you what they did with the rooms upstairs."

He keeps a straight face and follows me up the stairs to the second floor. Since the upper floors don't feature in the show, they didn't bother putting cameras up here. Especially since the construction company is still working on it.

As soon as we're in one of the rooms, Jud is on me, kissing me and running his hands everywhere he can reach. I can feel his erection against mine, but when I try to touch him, he goes down on his knees.

"Jud," I whisper.

"Shh. It'll be quick. I need it."

Damn right, it'll be quick. Looking at Jud's bright, lustful eyes as he licks his lips while taking my cock out is enough to get me almost there.

He runs his tongue from the crown all the way down to my balls, sucking on each while his hand grips my shaft, stroking it slowly but keeping it tight.

I bring my hand to my mouth to keep from moaning when he guides my cock into his mouth. There are hundreds of people downstairs, and the last thing we need is for anyone to know what we're up to.

I feel my orgasm build and try to warn him, but if I say anything, I know I'll give us away.

Jud strokes my shaft faster, keeping his mouth on my crown, ready to take my release. I put my free hand on his head to keep him in place as I come into his hot, wet mouth.

I'm still trying to recover when Jud stands up and kisses me, giving me a taste of my own release. He's hard against me, so I take his cock out and give it a few tugs.

"I'm close," he whispers against my mouth.

I bend down and suck him until his legs are shaking. I feel him grow even thicker in my mouth before his release hits the back of my throat.

We're both breathless, and our hair is all over the place, but fortunately, there's no other evidence of what just happened.

"Perfect crime," I say.

He leans against me, and I wrap my arms around him.

"Are you nervous?"

He nods.

"You didn't look like it downstairs."

"I'm the head chef. If they see me nervous, they'll get nervous. We're the first team they're working with, so they already have plenty to worry about without me adding to it."

"You're going to do great. You've come up with amazing recipes that incorporate the staple of our state. People aren't just trying new food here; they're coming home. Remember that."

He gives me another kiss, and we part. Time to get the show on the road.

I greet everyone as they come in before they're guided to their pre-booked tables. Because the change in lineup was made after bookings closed, we have a lot of diners who were coming to support the other team.

There are a few frowns and whispers, but as soon as they eat Jud's food, I see the change. They can't help but love it.

Each table has a spare seat for Yplanda. She hops from table to table to chat with the diners and see how they feel about the restaurant. Everything is captured by the cameras on the walls and numerous microphones.

She raises her hand to call me, so I head over to the table where she's sitting with a single person. A man wearing a suit and bowtie.

"Skyler, this is Patrick. He's visiting Vermont and booked a table specifically to try out your food, isn't that right?"

I hold out my hand to shake Patrick's. "Welcome to Maple Sky. I hope you're enjoying our selection."

"Hello, Skyler. I am enjoying it indeed. I was really intrigued when I read that Chef Judson Hale was part of this project. Can you tell me a little more about your concept?"

"Of course. I have to give Judson full credit for incorporating my own produced maple syrup into all of our recipes. You might not even know it's there in some dishes, but it really brings the flavors together. I produce maple syrup, but even I didn't know how versatile it could be. And the best thing is that you can even take one of our recipe cards home and try it for yourself."

"Thank you, Skyler. I think I will do just that. I'm torn between the maple-glazed turkey and one of the desserts. I have a sweet tooth, so it's probably quite unwise to take one of those recipes home."

I grab a recipe card box and put it on the table for Patrick before I leave him to check on everyone.

The rest of the night goes off in a flash, and soon we're saying goodbye to the last diners.

As soon as the restaurant door closes behind them, there's a loud cheer from everyone.

Jud comes out of the kitchen and runs to me, wrapping his arms around me in a tight hug.

"We did it. We did it."

"You sure did. Everyone loved your food," I say.

"No, *we* did it. Together. This wouldn't have been possible without all of us, plus the guys at Vino who banded together to help out."

Yolanda looks at her phone and smiles wide as she reads whatever is on it. She comes over to join Jud and me.

"This isn't standard practice, but after what I witnessed over the last few days and tonight, I feel I need to say something. I've never seen anyone put on a show so quickly and so well as you did. I just spoke to the Samantha and the producing team, who have been watching some of the footage live, and they're very impressed. Congratulations on your achievement today. We've kicked off the show with a bang, and I wish you all the best for the rest of the week and the competition."

Everyone claps, and then they start dispersing to clean up.

Yolanda turns to us.

"Guys, you've really outdone yourselves. Between you and me, the producers were shitting a brick when the other team had their accident, but you've pulled through and surprised them. As you know, the winners are decided by the diners who score the meal and the dining experience. I honestly wish you all the best, but I think you already stand a great chance of winning."

"Thank you, Yolanda. That means a lot," I say.

"And, Jud, your food really impressed Patrick Ludlow."

I smile, remembering the good-natured inquisitive guy from earlier, but when I look at Jud, he's gone pale, as if he's seen a ghost.

25

JUDSON

"Jud, are you okay?"

"I'll get him some water."

"Jud, baby, can you hear me?"

I look up at Sky, who's staring at me with worry plastered all across his face.

"Here," Yolanda says, pushing a glass of water in my direction.

I drink it. It doesn't taste right, but Yolanda looks relieved that I've drunk the water.

"Why don't you two get home? The production team will clean up and have everything ready for you tomorrow. You must be exhausted after the last few days."

I nod. "Thank you. You're right. I guess I didn't realize how much I was running on adrenaline. See you tomorrow?"

"You bet. I'm dying to try your mac and cheese with the maple-glazed bacon."

She gives us both a hug and virtually pushes us out the door.

I feel Sky's eyes on me as we walk over to his truck, but he doesn't ask me any questions, and the drive up to his cabin is also blissfully silent.

He leads me to the shower, and I allow him to take over for

me. My mind is too busy to instruct my body to do normal life things, and his gentle touch feels so good.

I know I shouldn't lean on him so much, but I can't help it, and I want to take all of it while I can. Before he decides I'm no longer good for him. Before he realizes that I destroy everything I touch.

Once we're both dry, Sky takes me to bed without bothering with clothes. I'm not in the mood for sex, and I can feel Sky isn't either, but his warmth against my body is everything I need right now.

"Do you want to talk, baby?" he asks gently.

I know I need to tell him, but my throat has my whole heart stuck in it. I'm not sure actual sounds will come out if I try.

"You went deadly pale when Yolanda mentioned that guy. Do you know who he is?"

I nod against his chest.

"He's the food critic that destroyed my career in Paris."

"Oh, Jud." He runs his fingers through my damp hair, and I try so bad to not cry.

"Sky, I'm so scared he'll give us a bad review again. He could damage your business before it even starts up."

"Our business."

"What? No, Sky. Aren't you listening? You can't be associated with me. And if Patrick is making an effort to follow me wherever I go, he'll destroy your reputation. I can't go to LA either."

"Now you're saying something that I like."

I look up at him. "What?"

He puts his hands on my face, cupping my cheek. "Jud, I don't want you to go to LA. I want you here in Vermont with me. I know it's selfish, and if you end up going to LA, I'll support you. I guess I'll need to save up for all the airplane tickets I'll need. But I need you to know that I want you here, in my life, in my bed, every day and every night."

I sigh. "I guess I could pick up more shifts at the bar. The pay isn't too bad for bar work, and I don't have many expenses, and with Pierre's money, I can set aside a rainy day fund."

Sky groans, and next thing I know, I'm looking straight into his hazel eyes while he pins me to the bed.

"Listen to every word I say, Judson Hale. You are an amazing chef. You are talented and creative, and the proof is in all the smiles I saw today, including Patrick's. He loved your food, so I have no doubt that he's going to give you a brilliant review. And whether we win the show or not, we'll work toward opening our restaurant. In some form or another, Maple Sky will exist. Also, I love you."

He swallows my gasp with his lips. I don't have a chance to reply or say anything else because he doesn't let me go for longer than it takes for me to draw a breath.

My dick hardens, and I feel his getting hard too, but they remain ignored in favor of more kissing, more tongue, more teeth. Fuck, I love kissing Sky so much.

Eventually we slow down as tiredness takes over and our kissing becomes slower. The passion is still there and, fuck me, there's so much love each time our lips meet.

Sky lies beside me, but his arms don't let me go, and I swear I fall asleep with his lips still pressed against mine.

The looming review is constantly on my mind. Even the celebration at the end of our week at the restaurant is bittersweet.

The kitchen team baked us a cake, and we're allowed to take home the large wooden restaurant sign that says Maple Sky.

To Sky's home, I mean. This place isn't my home, even though I've rearranged the kitchen to how I like it, and Sky didn't say anything. Quite the opposite. When he couldn't find something the other day, he seemed pleased to have to ask me where it was.

He hasn't repeated those words since that night, and I haven't said them back, even though I know I couldn't be more in love with Skyler West if I tried. I think I always have been.

But I'm terrified of saying it. I don't even know what I'm

waiting for, but the invisible force that's stopping me isn't letting go.

Instead, I take extra shifts at the bar, and I spend hours with my dad on the phone to lawyers in Paris, trying to figure out how to get away from Pierre.

Maybe that's it. I need to completely cut ties with Paris before I can move on.

I've decided to stay in Vermont, even though I haven't told Sky.

So that's where we are.

Waiting for something and doing nothing.

I spend every night with Sky, but I haven't moved any of my clothes to the cabin. My parents haven't asked me any questions, and even Luke has kept to himself.

There are so many unsaid things, and they're all so loud in my head and my heart that they may as well be a crowd with mega-phones all pointing in my direction.

I love Sky.

I'm staying in Vermont.

I don't know what I'm doing with the rest of my life.

Working right across from the restaurant is torture. Every night we get some diners spilling into Vino after their dinner, so I overhear how great the food is and how nice the new hosts are.

The production team couldn't have picked a more diverse set of contestants.

One team ran a grill with one single item on the menu, grilled steak, but they have over one hundred different sauces to go with it. I can see how that would be popular with the diners.

There was also a vegan restaurant, and toward the end of the competition, a team doing upside-down dinners where you start by having dessert and end with the appetizer.

While I doubt that the format would stick, it is definitely giving local people and visitors something to talk about.

Sky is confident about our efforts in the competition, but we were the first to go, and our week now feels like a million years ago.

Filming stopped last week, and we're getting the results today. There's a party at a secret location that only the contestants have been told about and sworn to secrecy because the show starts on TV this week.

Sky comes out of the shower, and my breath catches at the sight of him. And not because he's my giant, muscly Superman. No, my breath catches because today he's already done six hours of work at his parents' farm, packed his maple syrup to take to the stores he supplies tomorrow, and he still has a calm, happy smile when he looks at me.

"What?" he asks when he catches me staring.

Today his life could change for the best, and I think that for the first time in my life, I want to ask for something. I want my chance with Sky. My happy ever after.

My heart is beating so fast, I take a deep breath to steady it.

He drops his towel and puts on his underwear before stalking over to me. He holds my hands and walks backward until his legs hit the bed and he sits on it, taking me with him.

I straddle him and run my hands over his chest. His eyes are trained on my face, and I can see from the wrinkles on his forehead that he's trying to figure out what's inside my head.

This is it. This is the right moment.

"I love you, Sky. I didn't say it that night because I was too frightened that once I said it, I wouldn't have any more secrets. It didn't take me very long to figure out my sexuality because you were there with me like a guiding light. I think I loved you then. Even when I was all the way in Europe, my compass was always pointing west. I think my heart always knew that one day I'd be back, even if I didn't want to believe it. And I think I fell in love with you all over again that night at the bar when you saw me for the first time, and the first thing you did was smile."

"Jesus, Jud. You couldn't have just said *I love you too*."

He chokes, and I laugh.

"Apparently not."

26

SKYLER

I'm on top of the world as we leave the cabin to attend the award party.

The producers arranged a car to pick us up, which I'm thankful for because I can keep my hands on Judson the whole way there.

We're all dressed up because the whole thing will be filmed to show during the final episode, but right now, I couldn't care less about it all.

Judson Hale loves me. If I had a school book to write it on, I'd be scribbling away for the rest of the day.

Judson Hale loves me. Judson and Skyler forever. Judson loves Skyler.

I shake my head and reach out to Jud, who laces his fingers with mine.

"What are you smiling for?"

"Because the cutest boy in school loves me."

He laughs. "School was a long time ago."

"Doesn't matter. I still feel like I'm a teenager who was just asked to the prom by the guy he likes and never thought he stood a chance with."

"Are you kidding? You were Mister Popular at school. If anything, I was the one who never stood a chance," he says.

"Baby, you were the *only one* who ever stood a chance. Do you know I didn't lose my virginity until I was twenty-two?"

He gasps. "No way."

"I was waiting for you to come back. When I heard you had moved to Paris, I lost hope."

"Did you ever have a serious boyfriend?"

"Not really. There have been a few guys that I've hooked up with more than once, and a couple of short-lived relationships, but I've never let it get serious because I was too afraid to lose them like I lost you."

He squeezes my hand. "I really am sorry for leaving like that. It all seems so stupid now."

"Hey. None of that matters. Everything we did has brought us to this moment. I'd go through all that pain again knowing I'd be here now, holding your hand, and knowing you love me as much as I love you."

"I really do." He brings my hand up to his lips and kisses my palm. I take the chance to caress him. "We're finally getting somewhere with the accountant in Paris. They admitted that Pierre didn't actually tell them that he wanted to buy me out until a week ago. Sounds like they initially took his side but then were pissed off that he lied to us and made them look incompetent."

"That's great, babe. Soon you can leave all that behind and move forward…with me."

"What?"

"That wasn't very smooth." I chuckle. "Judson Hale, love of my life, will you move in with me?"

He smiles and tilts his head. "Are you asking only because you can't find anything in your kitchen?"

I shake my head. "I'm asking because even if my kitchen was bare, even if I'd never find the salt and pepper or sugar for my coffee, my life would still be complete just because I got to come home to you every day.

He laughs. "Skyler West. The ultimate romantic." And then he kisses me and nods his reply. "I think my mom will be happy for us."

I nod, knowing very well that my mom will be too. They'll be knitting baby clothes for us in no time if we're not careful.

The thought warms me up and makes me want all those things right now, so I don't voice them. We're both still young and have a dream business to start up before taking any further steps.

We arrive at the location of the party, a country house that could fit about two of my cabin in the front hall alone.

"Skyler. Judson. Welcome," Samantha, the producer, says as soon as she sees us. "Feel free to take a drink from the bar. We've pre-recorded the boring stuff, so we're ready for the announcement."

We find the makeshift bar and grab a drink before sitting at the table with our name cards. We wave at the other contestants. Unlike similar reality shows, we didn't mix with the other contestants. This show really is all about showcasing the best food Vermont has to offer.

Everyone goes silent, and the lights dim as Yolanda smiles at the camera.

"We've seen the best of the best and some unfortunate accidents. Sorry, Cornelia, I don't think any of us will ever look at cream the same way again."

There's laughter around the room, and a woman a few tables away from us blushes. We have no idea what happened during Cornelia's week, but I guess we're all playing along for the show.

"One thing we can be one hundred percent sure of, dear viewers, is that whoever wins this contest, the biggest winners are us, the public, who have met new culinary talent from our state, and hopefully, we'll see a few new restaurants opening soon."

An assistant goes on stage to hand Yolanda an envelope.

"Here it is. The envelope with the result. The names inside this piece of paper will have the pleasure of reopening their restaurant and running it lease-free for a whole year. The winning prize has been granted with the generosity of the town of Burlington, which is now replacing a burned building with a brand-new and exciting business. May this be a great example to many towns around the country. And without further ado..."

There's the sound of drumroll as Yolanda opens the envelope.

"The winners are...Judson Hale and Skyler West from Maple Sky."

There's a big round of applause, and I look at Jud, who's staring back at me as if he's waiting for someone else to stand up.

When the words settle in, he hugs me tight. "We won. Sky, we won!" Then he sits back. "Did I hear it right? There's no one with a similar name or something. Is this one of those Oscar moments when they read the wrong name?"

We hear Yolanda laugh. "I can assure you, Judson, I read the correct name. Why don't you both come on stage? We want to hear how you're feeling right now."

I stand up, and Jud follows, but before we leave the table, I reach to him and give him a kiss on the lips for everyone to see. Yep. Because by the time this is aired, I want everyone to know Jud is mine and I'm his. I stop short of beating my chest with my fists, but I like when Jud holds my shirt tight as I kiss him.

"And there you have it, folks. Confirmation that your suspicions were correct. Now come on up here, boys. We want to know everything."

We join her on the stage and answer her questions. It all seems surreal.

Jud hasn't let go of my hand since Yolanda announced our names, and it's just as well because I think I may float away if I'm not holding onto him.

After the interview, there's a small party, and we get to finally meet the other contestants properly. They're all really nice people and, not surprisingly, Jud finds a lot of common ground with the chefs from the other teams.

Before the end of the party, we're all told to sign NDAs agreeing not to talk about anything related to the contest results with anyone, including posting on social media. They have social media experts that post on our behalf while the show is being aired, so I don't worry about that.

As we're about to leave, Yolanda finds us.

"Hey, guys. I'm so pleased for you. You were a class act, and it's been a pleasure to do the show with you. Jud, I have something for you. The plan is to release this when you're officially announced winners and reopen Maple Sky, but Patrick said you could see it early."

She holds out a card, but instead of taking it, Jud holds onto me.

"Thank you, Yolanda. We'll open it at home if that's okay," I say, taking the card.

Jud is quiet on the way home, but I see his leg shaking repeatedly. I'm sure he has nothing to worry about, but I hold him during the car ride and wait until we're safely indoors.

He walks ahead of me, using the keys I insisted he keep and, for a moment, my heart is so full of happiness that everything has come together so perfectly.

"Will you read it?" he asks.

I take the card out. "The value—"

"No, not aloud. Read it first, and then tell me if I should see it. I don't want to be upset today."

I nod and look at the words printed on the card.

The value of knowing yourself.

I heard of Chef Judson Hale a long time before I had the chance to try his cuisine. Earlier this year, I happened to be in Paris, so I could not pass up the opportunity to visit Chef Hale's restaurant. My review was less than commendable, but while I stand by the words I wrote at the time, I also know when I'm not entirely right in my assessment.

A true good chef knows who he is. He's not just the combination of the skills he's taught at school or in the kitchen. The best chefs I've met all cook from the heart.

I am happy to say I had the chance to have seconds from Chef Hale—

pardon the pun—because, much to my delight, Chef Hale has now returned home.

What I tasted at Maple Sky was the essence of Vermont, and if you want to know what that is, I recommend you visit Maple Sky on Church Street in Burlington.

"Baby, I think you'll want to read this," I say.

He comes closer and takes the card from me.

I watch his face as months of self-doubt wash away with every word he reads. Everyone can agree Jud's cooking is the best, but I know this was important to him.

When he finishes, he throws the card up in the air and jumps into my arms.

I catch him and accept his hungry mouth.

"Come on, hotshot, take me to bed. All this stress has made me horny. Oh, let's go via the kitchen."

"I like how you think."

27

JUDSON

I've decided that the number one advantage of being Skyler West's boyfriend is that he can carry me around everywhere.

Oh shit! I'm Skyler West's boyfriend!

I know after the love declarations and his kiss in front of everybody earlier on, it's obvious we're not just dating. We're actual boyfriends. I mean, I agreed to move in and everything.

Is it possible to feel happier? I don't think so.

I'm sure I'll be pretty ecstatic in a few minutes, but even without that, even if we didn't have such an amazing physical connection, I'd still be the happiest man in the world. Sappy or what?

His hands are on my ass, and I'm most definitely happy for them to stay there, so I grab the bottle of Maple Sky from the counter and then get back to kissing him.

"Shit. Fuck," he shouts. "Just bumped my knee."

"This is why the best means of transportation is getting carried by someone else," I say, and then go back to sucking the skin on his neck because two can play this game.

"You know, for you to be carried, someone else has to do the carrying."

"Yup. Your point?"

He chuckles. "I like this Jud. I'll take all the versions available of Judson Hale, but I like this teasing carefree one."

"Well, I have plenty of reasons to be happy and carefree."

After a million years, we arrive at the bedroom, and I sigh when he drapes his body over mine on the bed.

"Hmm…naked," he moans against my lips.

"Yes."

Our hands are everywhere. I'm sure I undo some of the buttons on my shirt and some on his. I undo my fly, but then his hands are there, so I undo his.

His cock is heavy and leaking in my hand, and I've never wanted to have someone inside me so badly.

"Sky, I need you inside me, please."

He removes his lips from where they're sucking my ear lobe, and stares at me. I put a finger over his mouth. "Do it, and if you don't come, and I don't come, I'll top you after."

His bruising kiss claims me like a hot iron branding my heart.

"Mother of fucking maple taps, Sky. You kiss me like that, and there will be no topping, only a short-lived happy ending."

He sits back on his heels and removes the rest of my clothes and his before reaching over to his bedside table to grab two condoms and a small bottle of lube.

Sky may have never bottomed, but his experience topping makes it easy for me to relax and enjoy feeling his thick fingers stretching me.

By the time he's suited up and ready to get in me, I'm already on edge and desperate for more.

I'm glad when he doesn't ask me to turn over because I want to see his face every second of this. I want to know the moment when his forehead lines appear because he's trying to keep it together, because *that's* what I do to him. If that's not empowering, I don't know what is.

I cry when his head breaches the ring of muscles. The burn is real, but so is the incredible feeling of fullness that overcomes me.

"More, Sky. I need more," I beg.

"Baby, I'm not slowing down for you; I'm slowing down for me. Do you have any idea how tight you are? How I'm so ready to blow just watching you like this under me? You are stunning. Every single piece of you from your soft edges to your sexy tattoos, your amazing, caring heart."

He groans as I cant my hips to get more of him inside me.

"I need you to fuck me hard. I want to feel you tomorrow and every day after."

He does as I ask. Fortunately, his size makes it all borderline painful, so I know I won't come unless I touch my cock. And he seems to know that because he also leaves it alone.

I meet his eyes, and they're hungry. Hungry for more, hungry for me. I want to give him everything. What I couldn't give him before.

"Baby, your turn," I whisper.

He stops thrusting but stays inside me, catching his breath before he slides out slowly.

I remove his condom and discard it in the trash can by the bed. It's my turn to look after him.

"Just relax, okay? We'll go slow." I'm kneeling between his legs so I can see everything.

I add plenty of lube to my fingers and run them up and down his crease.

He wants this, but he's also clearly scared it'll hurt. It's written all over his face.

"Pass me the syrup," I ask.

His eyes go wide, and I laugh. "Don't worry, I'm not replacing lube with maple syrup."

With my free hand, I drizzle some syrup on his abs and his dick. I go in for the abs first because, hot damn, the man is ripped.

"Hmm, you taste good. So sweet." When his abs are thoroughly inspected, and I've decided they're the best abs in the world, I move on to my favorite dick. This one got the prize the first day I put my hands on it.

"Fuck." He bucks his hips when I suck his crown and doesn't

even notice I already have a finger inside him. I use the same strategy until he's cursing and riding my fingers.

"Jud…Jud…"

"Shh, I'll give you what you want, baby." I put the condom on and align my cock with his hole. I'm not as big as he is, but my fingers still aren't a match for my cock. "I need you to relax and breathe out as you bear onto me, okay? You're the one in control."

He nods and does as I say. He's so incredibly tight, and I'm not sure I can hold out for too long.

"You're doing so well. God, Sky, if you could see how beautiful you look with my cock half-buried inside you."

I push forward until I'm all the way in, and then he pulls me down so we're chest to chest. Our height difference means he needs to lift his head to meet my mouth, which also causes my dick to move inside him.

"Fuck, baby. That feels so good."

Maybe it's because we're both in awe of each other. Maybe it's because there are so many feelings swirling around us, but we last longer than I expected, and when I see Sky's tell-tale frown lines, I go for it, sitting up and thrusting to hit his prostate every time.

He comes, and I follow a moment later, spilling into the condom. We lie in bed catching our breath before we get enough energy to move over to the shower to clean up.

Luckily, none of the syrup made it onto the bed, so we get to fall asleep clean, sated, and in each other's arms like we should be.

I have a midday shift at the bar today, so I leave early to stop at my parents and pack some clothes so I can go straight to the cabin after my shift.

Sky has deliveries in Colebury and Tuxbury, so he's doing those before going to the farm.

It's all so domestic, and I love it. I love that we know what the other is doing, and we know we'll come back to the cabin at the end of the day.

It'll be even better when we get to work together at the restaurant. I try to not think about it too much so I don't give away our news to everyone at work.

"Mom?" I ask, going inside.

"Usual place, honey."

I go to the kitchen, where she's decorating cupcakes.

"Mom, I need to tell you something."

She puts her piping bag down on the table and goes to the sink to wash her hands.

"What's up, sweetie? Everything okay? You know...between you and..."

I love that she's totally not subtle about it, so I go over to her and give her a big smooch on her cheek.

"Everything is perfect. You probably already guessed it, but Sky and I have been...seeing each other."

She snorts. "Is that what the kids call it these days?"

"Mom!"

"Sorry, honey. Okay, tell me. I won't make fun of you."

"Would you be upset if I told you I'd like to move in with Sky? I'll still be close enough to see you all the time, and you could go there too."

She puts her hands on her chest, and I can see the emotion in her eyes. I think she's been waiting for this moment for as long as I have.

"Oh, Mom, don't cry. Just think of all the extra gossip you'll have with Mrs. W. You can exchange knitting patterns and make little jackets for the grandchildren you'll be asking us to give you in about six months, the whole nine yards."

"How old do you think I am, Judson Hale?"

I laugh and run away to my room before I get hit with a spatula.

With all my stuff packed in the car, I head over to the bar. I'm still early, so I plan to sit at the bar drinking soda and chatting to whoever is on the first shift.

The bar isn't too packed, so I don't feel bad for taking a seat. Molly sees me straight away and comes over.

"Hey, there's a guy with an accent asking for you. British, I think. I can never tell," she says.

"Where?"

She points to the booth on the opposite side of the bar.

My stomach sinks when I find myself staring at Pierre.

28

SKYLER

"Hey, Talia. I have your delivery for you."

The petite owner of Gourmont claps her hands when she sees the box in my hands.

"Ooh, thank you, thank you. I ran out last week, and people have been going nuts for it, especially after seeing you on TV."

I smile at her. It feels strange to be recognized, and I have to remember people are just now seeing stuff that was filmed weeks ago.

"That is so crazy. I'm only a sugarmaker. Jud's the chef, the one with all the talent. I hope people don't expect us to become some kind of crazy celebrities.

"Hmm...I'm not sure he's the only talent. Your Maple Sky was selling well enough before the show. Can you fix me up with four boxes next time you're out this way?"

"Sure. I can come by next week."

"Perfect."

I send her the invoice I have in my email drafts and make a note to bring her a new order next week. I also pick up a bag of dried herbs that my mom says are a pain in the butt to grow herself.

The next stop is Tuxbury, where I not only get a new bigger

order, just like Talia's, but the owner also gives me the card of a friend who has a store down in Rutland and would love to sell Maple Sky.

I can't believe the show hasn't even finished airing and it's already making a difference.

On my drive back to the farm, I decide that I'm going to have a conversation with my parents. I can't tell them we've won the show, of course, but it's no lie that I need to focus on my business.

I want to expand my tubing system so I can tap more trees. If my current demand continues this way, I will be close to running out of syrup before the next season.

And if I'm going to supply the restaurant, I definitely need to make sure I have enough syrup to cover that and my clients.

My phone rings, so I pull over to answer when I see Miles's name on the screen.

"Hey, Miles."

"Hey yourself. A little bird tells me you're shacking up with Judson Hale."

I laugh. "I didn't realize you were now part of the gossip mill."

"Hell no, if that gossip was turned into energy, we could power Burlington for a year. But you still haven't answered my question. Is Judson really back?"

"Yeah."

"Maaan, you're totally whipped. But Judson, really?"

"How can you tell that from a one-word answer? And yes, Jud. You know we've always been close."

There's silence on the other side.

"Skyler, I'm gonna say it straight because I'm your brother and I love you. I know how much you hurt after he left. I was there trying to pull you out of your head and back into the world. I don't want to see you like that again."

Miles's words feel a little sour. I know he's thinking of me, but Jud had a reason to leave. And just like Jud didn't have the whole story when he heard me talk to Blake, neither does Miles.

"I appreciate your concern, but we're not kids anymore. We're grownups, and we can deal with it. But I'm telling you, Miles, we're happy. Really happy."

"Kids or grownups, it hurts all the same. But I'm happy for you, Skyler. I'm looking forward to coming home and having a beer with both of you on your porch like old men."

I laugh. "Miss you, bro. Just another three months, and then you can whip Dad into shape. Can't wait to hear your ideas for the farm."

"Oh man, I have so many. We can implement so much to make the production more environmentally friendly and sustainable. And I want to use the land that isn't currently farmed or used for pasture."

"Wow, I really can't wait to hear more of your boring shit," I tease.

"Says the producer of liquid sugar."

"Hey, respect, I'm a TV star now."

He snorts.

"Hey, Skyler. Thank you. I don't know if I tell you this enough, but I really appreciate what you do. You're putting your life on hold for mine."

"The farm is our family, Miles. And family comes first. I'm looking out for your future the same way you would if the roles were reversed."

"Damn right I would, big brother."

We say our goodbyes, and I get back on the road, determined to make another big change in my life today. The farm comes first, but for the first time in my life, I finally see some wiggle room.

The house is silent when I open the dooryard, which is unusual unless my mom is in the garden because she likes to have the TV on in the background, or she's singing to herself.

I peek through the living room, and my dad isn't there either. Maybe he's back outside. His wrist has healed now, and even though he's supposed to be taking it easy, I wouldn't be surprised if he's out with the cows.

"Ma?" I call.

I hear the sound of a chair scraping the floor and go to the kitchen, where I see Mom in front of the sink with her head down and a paper towel in her hand.

"Ma? What's going on? Are you crying?"

She shakes her head, but when she looks at me, she breaks down.

I rush over and lead her back to the chair, grabbing the box of tissues from the top of the fridge and sitting next to her.

"Is everything okay? Where's Dad? Is he okay?" I start preparing for the worst. Not that anyone can ever be ready to receive bad news, but something must have happened because I've never seen my mom like this.

"He's okay. I told him to get out of my sight, so he's probably with the cows."

I take a deep breath, hoping this isn't what I think it is.

"What did he do?"

"What he always does. Sometimes I wish he was a cheater. If he was out there chasing women, I could handle that. But I don't know how to fight this...disease."

"How much?"

"Sixty grand."

As my mom cries into her tissue, I don't react. I must be in shock, or maybe I can't believe that I've heard her properly.

"Dad gambled sixty grand?"

She nods.

"How the fuck did he get his hands on sixty grand?"

"Apparently, he borrowed it from one of his gambling friends."

I stand up, and she doesn't stop me. Her eyes are tired. *She's* tired, just like me.

My dad is outside shifting manure, with Florrie watching him from a distance. The first milking of the day has been complete, so the rest of the herd is out in the pasture enjoying the nice weather and the green grass. I wish I could say the same for myself.

"Dad," I call.

He straightens up, sticking the pitchfork on the pile and rubbing his wrist.

"If you're coming to tell me what your momma said, you can turn back around. I heard it already."

"No, Dad, you haven't, because if you had, you wouldn't do something so stupid as gambling sixty fucking grand that isn't yours."

His face drops.

"Yes, Mom told me how much. And you know why? Because I've been doing your job since I was nineteen fucking years old. Mom and I are a team. We've had to become one to save our home and our family from your addiction. We've run the house and the business so we could put food on the table and keep a roof over our heads."

I try to keep my voice steady and avoid raising it, but it's damn hard. My dad is sick, and I have to remember that, but it doesn't mean he can't hear the truth. He needs to hear the consequences.

"Do you know how much I've given up for this place? I dropped out of college to work a job I never wanted to work. I've been stuck here all my life, waiting for the moment I can be free to live the way I want. Do you know how that feels?"

"Maybe if I had some control over this place, I wouldn't feel as if I'm being treated like a kid in my own home."

I laugh. "Dad, this place hasn't been yours since you gambled it away the first time. The bank loan that paid for your debt was in my name and the land has been in trust for Miles since he was sixteen to stop you from gambling away his future."

He stares at me.

"Dad. When are the excuses going to end? When are you going to have a good hard look at yourself and seek treatment? Why didn't you go see your therapist when you started having cravings again? Why didn't you say something? We're here to help and support you because, for some mysterious reason, we all love you. But right now, I can't be around you because you're the man who made my mom cry and has taken away the only thing I ever wanted."

I walk away from him and go back to the house.

My mom is still in the same spot as I left her. Still crying.

"Hey, Ma." I run my hand over her head, and she pulls me closer.

"I'm so sorry, baby. You shouldn't have to deal with this, any of this. I feel like we failed you so much."

"Hey, hey, none of that. Look at me, I'm smart *and* good-looking. That's all down to you. Besides, this isn't our first rodeo, right? We'll make it work."

She nods.

"I'll be back tomorrow, bright and early. Give Dad some space. I've given him a lot to think about."

"Don't worry about that. He's sleeping in the guest bedroom with the small couch. Maybe when his back hurts in the morning, he'll think twice about what he's done. That'll be a reminder of where he'll sleep for the rest of his days if he doesn't fix himself."

"That's my momma."

I give her a kiss and leave.

It's not until I'm at the end of the driveway that I decide I'm not going home. I need to see Jud, so I take the turn to Burlington.

The bar is busy, and I see Noah and the guys at a small table close to the door.

I haven't seen them for a while, between the season, the show, and working the farm and market, not to mention the time I've been spending with Jud. I've missed all of our usual boys' nights.

"Hey, guys." I pull up a chair and sit next to Noah.

"Hey, look who it isn't," Wyatt says.

"Well, he sure can't be our friend, Skyler, because he's too busy to hang out with his friends," Andy adds.

"Screw you," I say, and Wyatt and Andy give each other a heated look. "Ew. Noah, make it stop."

I look at the bar and can't see Jud or an opening to grab a drink anytime soon, so I grab Noah's cider and take a sip.

He gives me a *how dare you* look but then leans close.

"When's Judson leaving? I thought you still had to be free to film the live interviews after the show ends."

"What?"

The fuck is he talking about? Oh, he must have overheard Jud saying he's moving out of his parents' place.

"Tonight. He's packed already."

"Wow, really? What's he doing here? Shouldn't he be at the airport already?"

Airport?

My face must have shown confusion because Andy leaned over the table.

"He was talking to a guy earlier about going back to Paris. He has a restaurant there or something about expanding a restaurant. I'm not sure, they were whispering, and I didn't want to look like I was spying on them."

I'm lost for words. Jud is going to Paris?

"What I don't get is why the guy had a British accent but sometimes spoke in French," Wyatt says. "You think that's how it is in Europe? They all speak each other's language? Also, French-speaking Judson is H.O.T."

"Um, guys, I have to go. Just remembered I need to pack up an order to deliver in the morning. I'll see you all around."

I walk out of the bar and manage to keep it together until I get to my truck.

My legs feel weak as if I've had the rug pulled out from under me, and I'm falling to the ground in slow motion.

A few hours ago, my future was at the tips of my fingers, within my grasp, and now I feel like I've gone back ten years. Somehow, after everything that happened today, I stupidly thought that Jud and I were also a team. Maybe our dream would take a little longer, but we'd make it work.

Now I can see that wasn't his dream at all. I wasn't his dream.

I put the truck in gear and drive to the cabin.

Time to take back my life.

29

JUDSON

Ugh, this is like the shift that never ends.

All I want to do is go home, but since someone called in sick and there was no one else available, I volunteered to stay on.

It's the least I can do after all the support I've had from the team, but damn, today is really not the day for this.

"Excuse me. Hey, bar person." I turn to the jackass, who thinks he's better than us, and give him my best smile.

"Yes, sir. How may I help?"

"You can help by making sure I'm getting the wine I've paid for. I asked for a large glass of red Merlot, and that girl over there only filled it halfway."

I know Molly didn't underfill the glass because that's not something I've ever seen her do, but I don't want him to make a scene and upset her, so I take the bottle and fill up the glass to what it was before he drank some of it.

"Now that's better. I don't understand why someone would hire a female bartender at a gay bar. Now, you…" he drawls. "I'd stare at fifty of you all day long."

I don't want to be rude, but this guy is escalating fast, and I'm not sure I can contain myself.

Tanner appears next to me as if I called Beetlejuice three times in my head.

"Good evening, sir. Is everything okay with your drink?" he asks.

The guy looks Tanner up and down, focusing on his tattooed arm. Tanner is gorgeous and has this whole broody thing going on, but he's in a committed relationship, and I can tell by the tick in his jaw that he's not enjoying being appreciated.

"I was saying to your colleague here that I think—"

Tanner stares the man down. "I heard what you said. To answer your question: this isn't a gay bar, this is an inclusive bar. We welcome everyone regardless of their gender, sexual orientation, or identity, but we do draw the line at creepy assholes, so I guess maybe we're not that inclusive after all. Drink your wine, and don't make me have to walk you out."

Both the man and I are in shock but for different reasons. Tanner taps my elbow and gestures for me to follow him to the back.

"Everything okay?" he asks.

"You're asking *me* that?" I laugh, and he shrugs.

"Thanks for staying on tonight. It's busy out there, and I know you probably want to head home since you missed Skyler earlier."

What? *Sky was here*? *When*?

"Um, thanks, Tanner. It's not a problem, and thanks for that." I tilt my head toward where the man was sitting. "He was upsetting Molly."

He nods and leaves to go clear tables.

After working with so many chefs and restaurant managers who didn't lift a finger outside of their responsibilities, it's refreshing to see Tanner working with us and not just overseeing things.

By the time I make my way to the cabin, it's too late for Sky to be up, but the thought that I can just cuddle up to him and without waking up he'll pull me to his chest almost makes me want to break speed laws.

On the drive, I think about my conversation with Pierre. I want to put all of that behind me before I start my life with Sky.

I still can't believe Pierre came all the way to Vermont to convince me to go back to Paris.

"But, darling, we were such a great team," he'd said.

"From where I stood at the door to our bedroom the night you were supposedly sick with the flu, you had found yourself a new teammate," I'd bit back, but his reaction showed little if no remorse.

I hadn't wanted to discuss his betrayal because I was past it and starting to consider that me catching him, as much as it hurt at the time, was for the best. I hadn't been in love with him.

I'd been in love with my restaurant and my career because I didn't have anything else.

And that was the deciding factor.

The only place in the world that I belong is wherever Sky is, and I am no longer tied to my warped concepts of belonging, achievement, or even love.

In the end, Pierre accepted that he'd wasted the trip because I wasn't going to go back to Paris with him. He emailed his accountant right there and then to request the release of the funds and to transfer the full ownership of the restaurant to him.

The money isn't important to me anymore, but I know it gives Sky and me a good safety net. Maybe we can get his pipelines installed before next winter so he'll be able to increase his production for the next tapping season.

I'm surprised to see light coming from the living room window as I approach the cabin. My body almost vibrates with the anticipation of finding Sky awake. Maybe we can have a shower together before we cuddle in bed.

My cock hardens at the thought, and I feel happy that this is my life now.

I don't even bother unloading my stuff from the car. I can do that in the morning.

Everything is quiet when I walk in. I find Sky in the living room.

There's an empty glass on the coffee table and a half-empty bottle of scotch.

"Sky, baby. What happened?"

He looks up slowly as if he's surprised to see me.

"What are you doing here?"

"Baby, I live here. You asked me to move in. Have you been drinking?"

He snorts. "I'm drinking because I can. That's what adults do. We can make decisions for ourselves. At least when *I* make a decision, I stick to it."

"Sky, I don't understand what you're trying to tell me. Come on, let's get you in the shower." I get closer, but he moves to the other side of the couch.

"Shouldn't you be at the airport? Flying to Paris to go back to your little boyfriend that speaks two languages and probably wears branded fancy clothes? Now that you have what you want, there's nothing holding you back."

What the hell?

"Sky, I don't know how you found out that Pierre was at the bar, but it's not what you're thinking."

"Did he ask you to go back to Paris?"

"Yes."

"Did he talk about expanding your business?"

"Yes, but—"

He raises his hand to interrupt me, but I don't stop.

"No, Sky. Don't tell me to shut up. You're asking me what he wanted, but you're not giving me a chance to tell you my answers. Do you even want to know what I told him?"

"It doesn't matter. You should go to Paris anyway because there's nothing here for you."

What?

"Sky...what are you saying?" I feel like he's sticking a knife through my gut, about to twist it for good measure before leaving me to bleed to death.

"I can't open Maple Sky. I'm going to work at the farm and help out Miles when he comes back."

"Why?"

"Because my dad fucked up my life again, and I have no choice. I have no fucking choice." He's shouting, but I know he's not shouting at me. We've talked about his dad's addiction before, and I know how much he tries not to resent his dad.

"Sky, I can help. Pierre—"

"Go home, Jud. Leave and go somewhere you can follow your dreams and do something with your life. There's nothing in Vermont but disappointment and shackles tied to fucking heavy rocks."

"Sky, please. Let's talk this through. We can solve this together."

He laughs.

"You left me once because of what you thought you heard. I'm not going to sit here waiting for the day you come to the realization this is not what you want and you leave again. I'm done with everyone else running my life and my heart. From now on, if my life goes to shit, then it goes to shit on my own terms."

"That's not fair, Sky."

"Life isn't."

I don't understand what's happening right now, but there's one thing I do know.

"If you don't already know what I want, Sky, then maybe my place really isn't here."

I turn around and leave, hoping my parents are already asleep so I don't have to talk to anyone because I don't think I can.

I try to make sense of things, but it's too hard to separate Sky's hurtful comments and the other stuff he told me.

His dad gambled again. Okay, but why can't we have Maple Sky and expand his business? Isn't Miles coming back soon?

My head hurts, and I just want to get under a blanket and cry.

When I look at my phone to set my alarm for the morning, I see the photo I took of Sky and me in Tuxbury. I was trying to take a nice photo, but at the last minute, he licked my face, so we ended up with this weird photo of my scrunched-up face with his tongue flat on my cheek.

I ran once when I misunderstood the situation, but I'm not running again. When we can have a sober conversation, if he still doesn't want me, if he still doesn't trust me to look after him the way he looks after me, then I will accept that we're over.

Until then, whether he likes it or not, he's mine. But I do hope he wakes up tomorrow with a killer hangover for making me sneak into my parents' house in the middle of the night rather than cozying up to my boyfriend after a good orgasm.

30

SKYLER

My head is killing me, and my bladder insists that I need to get up.

I reach over to complain to Jud about the unfairness of my life, but he's not there.

Everything comes rushing back at the same time my stomach decides it doesn't like me, and I barely make it to the bathroom before I throw up.

I empty my bladder and then reach out for the toothbrush and mouthwash.

Jud's toothbrush is there right next to mine.

I ignore it because I can't think about last night yet. Not before I have a shower and coffee.

And because I'm a coward who's afraid he's screwed up all the good things in his life, even after the shower and coffee, I still avoid thinking about what I said to Jud. How I pushed him away.

He's probably on a one-way flight to Europe to follow his dreams while I'm still stuck here.

Dammit. So much for not thinking about it.

I get in my truck and drive to the farm

When I arrive, I hear noise in the barn, so I know my dad isn't in the house. I don't particularly want to spend any time with him today, so I go in the house to say hi to my mom first.

"Morning, honey. I made you pancakes."

"Hey, Ma." I kiss her on the head and sit at the table. My mom's cooking must be magic because my stomach has decided to get up for pancakes. She puts a cup of fresh coffee in front of me and sits down at the table.

"I did a lot of thinking last night after you left," she says.

"Uh-oh, are these pancakes safe?"

She hits me on the shoulder, and I laugh, but then she becomes serious.

"Skyler, I don't want you to put your life on hold anymore. I want you to follow your dreams with Judson. It's not fair to ask you to pause your business, especially when it's growing so well. Whatever happens with this TV show, I think you could still open your restaurant with Jud. You've been talking about it since you were little boys."

I give her a resigned smile. "Ma, it's not that simple. When Dad's friend comes to collect, we'll need to have the money, and at the moment, we don't. The mortgage on my land is paid, so if I go to the bank, I'll get a loan, and all we need to do—"

"No, Skyler. I would rather lose the farm than have you risk your business. But it won't happen anyway because I found a solution."

"What do you mean?"

"I called Miles yesterday after you left. I know you take the burden of the farm on your shoulders, but he is the legal owner, and now that his finals are over, even if he's not here yet, he needs to be part of the decision-making process. We talked it through, and he suggested selling part of the land to the next-door neighbor."

"But you never wanted to sell it. You said it was part of our heritage."

"That was before. Miles always wanted to have enough land to split with you if you wanted to live there, but then you bought the forest and the cabin."

I almost can't believe what my mom is saying, and yet, it makes perfect sense.

All of these years, I wanted to preserve the farm for my brother and got used to making decisions for everyone. I don't even think I realized how much of a burden that was until now.

I let out a breath of relief and almost want to cry.

My mom hugs me tight.

"You've been the best son and big brother this family could have ever wished for, but it's time for you to look after yourself. Maybe even let someone else step in every once in a while."

I nod in her embrace.

"Dad is going to see his therapist next week. He knows he's on a very short leash with me. God knows how much I love that man, so I'm not letting his addiction steal him from us."

"Mom, I did something really stupid. I pushed Jud away last night. I said some awful things."

She puts her hands on my face.

"Yesterday was a difficult day for all of us. We're allowed to make mistakes and even say the wrong things. Why don't you go talk to him and make nice?"

"Can I do it now?"

"Of course you can, baby."

I hug her and run out of the house.

I try to call Jud, but he's not answering his phone, and when I get to his parents' place, there's no one home either. My anxiety spikes, and my fear that he's gone to the airport becomes real.

"Okay, calm down, Sky," I say to myself.

My computer is at the cabin, so I drive there, mentally checking if I have enough money in my account to buy a ticket to Paris. I don't even know how much a ticket to Paris is. Is my passport still in date? Fuck.

Jud's car is parked in front of the cabin when I get there. I run inside, not even bothering to close the door to my truck.

"Jud," I call out while I search for him.

I find him in the bedroom by the chest of drawers with a pile of folded clothes in his hand.

He puts them in the drawer and shuts it. Were those his clothes?

My heart does a little happy jolt.

"Jud—"

"Your turn to listen to me. I don't care what you think you heard or what you believe. I know you love me, Skyler West, and I know that you know I love you. When you love someone, you talk to them and tell them your problems. You resolve them together. Do you know why I left Paris? Why I didn't try to resolve things with Pierre?"

I shake my head.

"Because I didn't love him. Not like I love you. There was nothing to save."

He comes closer, and my hands twitch with the need to touch him.

"We deserve to be together, Sky. I can help pay whatever debt your dad is in. The money from the restaurant should be in my account in a few days. I don't need it. Everything I need is right in front of—"

I stop him by slamming my mouth onto his for a searing kiss. He wraps his arms around me and kisses me back until we're both breathless.

"I love you so much, baby, and I'm so sorry about what I said last night. I didn't mean any of it."

"Yes, you did. You were protecting yourself, and you were protecting me like you always do."

My throat feels so tight that all I can do is nod.

"So, here's how this is going to work," he doesn't let go of me but points out to the closet. "I've taken up half of your closet, and you're getting the lower drawers on the dresser because I want to look at your ass every time you bend down to take a shirt out."

"I think I can live with that," I say, and then walk him back toward the bed slowly, removing my shirt and his without taking my mouth off of him.

He lies on the bed, and I follow, pulling down his jeans, underwear, and socks until he's fully naked.

My mouth waters at the sight of his hard cock, heavy against his belly. I get rid of the rest of my clothes and kneel between his legs. I suck his balls into my mouth, hearing his intake of breath when I tug them with my teeth.

I run my tongue down his crease and suck his hole. My cock is hard and hanging heavy, jolting with every curse word out of Jud's mouth, every caught breath.

When I'm happy that he's relaxed enough, I search out a condom and lube and sheath my neglected cock. I'm wound so tight that even putting the condom on feels too good.

Jud grabs the bottle of lube from my hands and squirts some onto his fingers.

I'm lost for words at the sight of him readying himself for me with the same desperation I feel.

"I want to ride you."

I sit up and grab some pillows to place behind my back before leaning against the bed frame. Jud straddles me, and without any warning, impales himself on my cock.

"Fuck," I cry while he lets out a moan.

I put my hands on his hips, but he doesn't want to go slow as he lifts his hips up and slams down on me again.

"Sky, god, you feel so good."

"This isn't going to last, baby."

"Oh, yes it will because we can keep on doing this over and over again, Sky. Every day, every night, for the rest of our lives.

His words are a claiming stake on my heart, and my body reacts by letting go. He brings his hand to his cock and strokes himself until he's spilling all over my chest.

His channel grips my dick tighter as he's coming, and it's like a ripple of aftershocks straight onto my cock.

He falls onto my chest, breathing heavily. I wrap my arms around him feeling his heartbeat under my touch.

Will sex between us always be like this? I can't wait to spend the rest of my life finding out.

31

JUDSON

I stare at the coffee in front of me. Steam rising up and transporting the scent of the bitter, dark roast.

Was it only eight months ago that I sat at my parents' kitchen table, holding a similar cup of coffee and feeling so lost and broken?

How can so much change in such a short time?

Sky leans against the kitchen doorframe, wearing nothing but a towel around his waist.

I sit back in the chair and take a sip of my coffee.

"You know better than to put yourself between a man and his need for caffeine," I say.

He does this thing where he lowers his head and then looks up, making those sexy ripples on his forehead appear. The man is evil.

I shake my head.

"You know I love you, right?" he says.

"I think I got the message earlier when you were balls deep inside me shouting your release into my ear. I may need to see a doctor."

I take another sip of the coffee. This new roast we're sampling for the restaurant is amazing.

"Are you going to stand there looking gorgeous all day? In case you haven't noticed, today is a pretty big deal," I say.

"How big?" he asks.

I look down and see his dick straining against the towel.

"Huge."

He snorts and turns around to go back to the bedroom.

I put the coffee down and chase after him.

He already knows me so well because, when I turn into the bedroom, I run straight into his chest.

His arms come around my waist.

"I knew you couldn't resist me," he says, kissing the tip of my nose.

"You are pretty irresistible...but as irresistible as you are, we need to leave shortly." I cup his erection. "Save this for later."

We arrive at the restaurant somewhat later than I would have liked, thanks to Mister Washboard Abs making a show of getting dressed.

The final episode of the show is being aired tonight, and tomorrow, the boards that went up again after filming will be removed to show the plaque above the window that says Maple Sky.

We will also start welcoming diners tomorrow. But tonight is special because we were allowed to tell our close friends and family that we won, and they're coming to the restaurant for a special dinner and to watch the finale.

It's been a busy few months recruiting the right people to work in my kitchen and up front. We've also fully redecorated the restaurant, so there's a display of maple-related foodstuff available for sale.

Sky's maple syrup and cream are, of course, the stars of the show.

Yesterday, we collected the menus and recipe cards from Imprescott Designs, who is giving us a special rate because we're changing our menus every six weeks. They'll be getting regular orders from us. Plus, they're a local business, which makes it even better.

With Sky's help and knowledge of the local farmers, we're able to offer one hundred percent local fare. Even our pasta is made using flour from a local mill.

"How's everything backstage?" Sky asks through the open window into the kitchen. That was another addition from us. I always like to see the action from the kitchen when I dine out, so I wanted to offer the same experience.

"All good. The team is ready to serve. Wanna go upstairs with me to help me wash my hands?"

He smiles and gives me an almost imperceptible nod.

We both run up the stairs and into one of the classrooms.

As soon as the door closes behind us, Sky is on me. There's no time for rushed blowjobs, but I needed a moment with him.

"I can't believe this is really happening," I say.

"Me neither. I can't even fry an egg, and now I own a restaurant."

I laugh.

"I've worked in prestigious kitchens, and I know for a fact some of my colleagues would definitely look down on us, but I've never been so proud of anything in my whole life. More than that, I get to do this with you, and I wouldn't change that. For me, this is the most prestigious job I'll ever have."

"Come on. Let's go downstairs and greet our fans. I believe we promised free food, so knowing Miles, he won't have eaten since yesterday at breakfast."

"Let's do it."

I do one last check in the kitchen before joining Sky, who's letting everyone inside.

My parents and Luke all come over to me, hugging me tight.

"Does this mean I get free food anytime?" Luke asks.

"Do you know how to wash pots?"

"Ugh, you're as bad as Mom. *No cake unless I help clean the kitchen*," he says, mimicking our mom.

"What can I say? I had the best teacher."

They take a seat at the table. We arranged it to be a circle with a gap in the middle to make it easy for the waiters to bring the food and for everyone to see each other. After the dinner, we'll move everything to the restaurant setup.

I sidle up to Sky, who's holding Ollie.

"Hey, little dude. Don't steal my man, and I'll give you a lollipop, okay?"

Anita laughs. "That ship sailed about five minutes after I gave birth."

I look at Sky and see a little blush appear on his neck.

"You know how you feel soooo attractive while pushing a melon-sized thing out of your hoo-hah, and your husband is standing there looking at you adoringly as if he's ever going to forget that moment?"

"Can't say I've experienced that, but go on," I say.

"Well, it wasn't just my husband standing there."

"Noooo."

"Yup. And he insisted on taking his shirt off and bonding with the baby too."

I raise my brows. "Babe, I feel this is information we should have disclosed before."

He looks at Ollie and rubs his tummy. "Don't listen to the grownups. You'll always be my best friend," he coos.

There's a collective shake of heads, and when I spot Sky's mom sitting next to mine, I point at them. "No ideas, you two."

Sky hands Ollie back to Anita and grabs a highchair before following them to their seat.

The bar crew can't all be here because the bar is open, but they promised to take turns dropping by, so I have instructed the team to have plated snacks for them.

When everyone is settled, Sky and I remain standing.

He gives me a peck on the lips, and then we face our family and friends.

"It feels unbelievable that we're here today, and still, in some ways, it's like this was always meant to be. Life has given us all our fair share of challenges, but it has also given us plenty of strength and resilience to face them all together as a family."

As I say the words, I see Sky looking at his dad, who's been on his own journey.

"There's someone out there who almost thirty years ago placed our moms on the same maternity ward. A friendship that stemmed from sharing such a special moment has survived the test of time. Is it any surprise that Sky and I ended up together?"

Everyone laughs.

"Anyway, enough of the mushy stuff," Sky says. "Let's try some awesome food. I know the chef, he can be a pain in the butt, but his food is great."

There's more laughter as we sit down, and the waiters start serving the appetizers.

A few hours later, we all enjoy dessert as we watch the show's final episode on a TV screen brought into the restaurant just for the purpose.

Everyone toasts to us and the future of our business, and a little while later, we're back to being just us and our team.

We both take a deep breath and smile stupidly at each other. We don't need more words.

"Come on. I want to take you somewhere," he says.

SKYLER

"You what? Babe, it's late, and we have to clean up."

I hold his hand and bring it up to my mouth for a kiss.

"We're off cleaning duty. I've organized it with the guys," I say.

"When?"

"When I decided that I wanted to take my boyfriend home for much-deserved nooky."

He laughs. "You didn't just say that."

"Oh, he did," Carly, the sous chef, shouts from the kitchen. "You better take him out of here before we need to bleach our ears and eyes as well as all the kitchen surfaces.

Jud follows me to the staff room. We grab our things and get in the car.

"Um, babe...this isn't the way home," he says when he finally realizes I missed our turn ages ago. He's so busy talking about the different coffee roasts we can stock, he isn't paying attention.

"I know."

"Where are we going?"

"You'll find out soon."

I take his hand and place it on my thigh. He turns it around and laces his fingers with mine.

Today has been truly unbelievable, but I'm starting to accept that most days I spend with Jud are unbelievable.

In just a week, we're getting a delivery for my new pipelines, so while Jud heads off to the restaurant earlier in the day, I'll be spending some time clearing the forest to make it accessible.

I can't believe that I'll be tapping the whole of my forest this winter. It should stress me out, but I no longer feel the need to do everything on my own.

Miles has volunteered to help because he's interested in the process, and I can now afford to hire someone to help.

When Miles came back, he didn't come alone. It seems that, along the way, my little brother fell in love with the daughter of the owner of the farm he was working at.

Steph is a great girl and hit it off with my mom straight away. Together they're increasing the production of their chutneys and jams and have taken over my spot at the farmer's market.

I'm a little sad that I no longer have time to do it regularly, but as long as Maple Sky is available for their customers, everyone's happy.

"Wait, is this..." Jud starts.

"It is."

"Why are you bringing us here?" I look at him after parking

the car. He's frowning. I get it because, after all, McKenzie Park doesn't hold the best memories for either of us.

"We're replacing a bad memory with a good one." I step out of the car and go around to meet him.

We walk hand-in-hand to the exact spot that has the rock we sat on that night.

I guide Jud to the rock. He sits on it, and I kneel between his legs, taking both his hands in mine.

"Jud, I once thought that my land and my house were the only things that were truly mine. They were the place I set my roots, and they would help me grow and make me solid. I was wrong. You, Judson Hale. You are all that and more. You are my stronghold, and I will defend us for as long as I live. One day I'm going to ask you to marry me. And I hope that on that day, you will know that I love you then more than I love you now and that I've loved you since I was old enough for my heart to beat for another person."

"Why don't you ask me now?" he asks, and I can see his eyes shiny with unshed tears.

"Because I'm an airhead who forgot the rings."

"So when you say you'll ask me one day…"

"I mean later, baby. I'll definitely ask you later."

"Can I tell you yes right now? Because it'll still be a yes later, tomorrow, next month, next year, until forever."

THE
END

ACKNOWLEDGMENTS

It's been a pleasure and a privilege to write in Sarina's World of True North. I cannot thank Sarina and her team enough for picking my story to be part of this amazing world.

Writing is usually a solitary activity, but Stronghold was ninety percent written while on video calls with Rhys Everly-Lawless, who has been a constant source of goodness in my life from the moment we met.

I also want to thank my alpha readers, Tanya and Lisa and my beta reader, Anka. These three women are a constant source of reassurance, but never afraid to tell it as it is.

To all the readers that have given my stories a chance, who've walked into the worlds I created and had a good time there... thank you. You're the reason I get to be an author every day for the rest of my life.

Finally, I need to thank my partner, Froglet.

When we sat on the tiled floor of the empty living room of our new house, I told him I'd like to take a year off work to focus on my writing. We'd just used all our savings. But he didn't bat an eyelid. A year after that, I became a full-time author.

Through all of life's challenges, just like Judson and Skyler. we are each other's stronghold.

Ana

xx

Printed in Great Britain
by Amazon

38321244R00116